Advance Praise for
Fly Back, Agnes

"I love Elizabeth Atkinson's novels for their emotional complexity and the sensitive but frank portrayals of tween and preteen protagonists. *Fly Back, Agnes* is a beautifully written, deft, imaginative portrayal of a girl on the cusp of becoming herself and discovering her own powers. From the first word to the last, Atkinson's narrative voice stays unswervingly true to her narrator, the eponymous Agnes, in a way that will resonate deeply with all readers, and especially younger ones."

—Kate Christensen, PEN/Faulkner award-winning author of *The Great Man* and *The Last Cruise*

"*Fly Back, Agnes* settles right in your heart. The storytelling holds you tight with secrets abounding all round."

—Terry Farish, author of *The Good Braider* and *Either the Beginning or the End of the World*

"*Fly Back, Agnes* is a charming novel that I read in one sitting. Elizabeth Atkinson has crafted a quirky yet tender story that also manages to explore some of the deep challenges faced by today's youth. I loved this book and am ready to pack my bags and head off to rural Vermont!"

—Laurie Friedman, author of the Mallory series

"Elizabeth Atkinson has written a tenderhearted coming-of-age novel that gives you all the feels—each character as intriguing and multilayered as the next."

—Danielle Joseph, author of *Shrinking Violet*, *Indigo Blues*, and *Pure Red*

"Agnes's story is full of revelations. The truth is delicate and durable—and different than it appears."

—Blythe Woolston, author of *MARTians*

Fly BACK, AGNES

Elizabeth Atkinson

Carolrhoda Books
Minneapolis

Carolrhoda Books®
An imprint of Lerner Publishing Group, Inc.
241 First Avenue North
Minneapolis, MN 55401 USA

For reading levels and more information, look up this title at www.lernerbooks.com.

Jacket illustration by Julie McLaughlin.

Main body text set in Bembo Std.
Typeface provided by Monotype Typography.

Library of Congress Cataloging-in-Publication Data

Names: Atkinson, E. J. (Elizabeth Jane), 1961– author.
Title: Fly back, Agnes / by Elizabeth Atkinson.
Description: Minneapolis : Carolrhoda Books, Lerner Publishing Group, [2020] |
    Summary: Twelve-year-old Agnes hates everything about herself, starting with her
    name, so while spending a summer with her father, a cellist, she decides to become
    someone else.
Identifiers: LCCN 2019006852 | ISBN 9781541578203 (th : alk. paper)
Subjects: | CYAC: Identity—Fiction. | Self-acceptance—Fiction. | Family problems—
    Fiction. | Divorce—Fiction. | Cello—Fiction. | Musicians—Fiction.
Classification: LCC PZ7.A86373 Fly 2020 | DDC [Fic]—dc23

LC record available at https://lccn.loc.gov/2019006852

Manufactured in the United States of America
1-46902-47805-10/22/2019

For Nate, Madeleine, Erik, and Obi too

"Two roads diverged in a wood, and I—
I took the one less traveled by,
And that has made all the difference."

—Robert Frost

Chapter 1

I was surrounded by racks and racks of swimsuits, as if circled by sharks.

"Mo, do we have to do this now?" I asked my mom. Everyone calls her Mo, which is short for Maureen.

"Come on," said Mo, waving at the counter for assistance like she was landing an airplane. "This is the perfect way to celebrate the end of the school year."

I wasn't in the mood to celebrate. Yesterday had been my last day at Pico Primary, the only school I had ever known. In the fall, I would be moving over to the enormous regional middle school, along with hundreds of other new seventh graders from all over Kettleboro, Vermont. Just thinking about the maze of hallways and a confusing cafeteria in that gigantic cement building made my stomach cramp.

"I already told you, I don't want a new—"

"What can I help you with, ladies?" the saleswoman chirped as she fluttered across the store.

I crossed my arms and scowled.

"This is the first day of my daughter's summer break," announced Mo, "and she needs a bathing suit. Nothing too pricey. Just a cute, sporty number that shows off her new curves."

My face instantly burned.

"Ooh, let's think about this," said the saleswoman, staring at me as if I were a mannequin in the window. "I would love to find something to complement those gorgeous exotic tones."

"Exotic" was supposed to be the nice way of describing the way I looked, but that word made me cringe. I'd inherited my dad's tawny skin and piercing dark eyes, tossed together with Mo's genes—her coiled, copper hair and excessive freckles. The combination makes it hard for people to label me, no matter how hard they try. And in the white world of Kettleboro, they try a lot.

Within minutes, Mo had gathered a dozen suits.

"Let's get this over with," I grumbled as I grabbed the hangers and trudged toward the dressing rooms.

Halfway across the store I overheard the saleswoman ask, "So she's adopted?"

No one ever thought I could hear that question, but I always heard, even when they didn't come right out and say it.

"Nope," Mo whispered loudly, as if everyone in the entire world needed to know, "her dad's half Korean and I'm mostly Scottish with a dash of Lebanese on my paternal grandfather's side."

Sometimes I wish I had been adopted. That would explain a lot.

Reluctantly, I tried on the first suit and stared at myself in the three-way mirror. Part of me still believed that one day I would wake up and find myself as I used to be, scrawny and shapeless. But standing under the fluorescent lights, in a navy blue one-piece, I looked curvier than ever.

"Can I see?" Mo called from the other side of the curtain. "I bet that orange one with spaghetti straps is sensational."

"This is a waste of time. I don't even like swimming anymore."

"Hang tight," my mother commanded. "I'll check the racks again."

I ignored her and changed back into my clothes.

"Nothing for you, sweetie?" asked the saleswoman as I handed her the pile of rejects.

I shook my head and found Mo by the bikinis. She held one in front of me, pastel pink and lacy.

"Not a chance," I hissed, and we finally left.

×××

We stopped for lunch at Mo's favorite café, Pita Pan, in the center of Kettleboro, and were seated outside under a striped umbrella.

As soon as we'd ordered, Mo leaned in too close to my face. "Did you take a look at that book from the library I left on your bureau? The one on *becoming a woman*?" She grinned hard like she always does when explaining the facts of life, as if we were in on a wonderful secret together.

Mo had given the *becoming a woman* lecture so many times, I knew it by heart. Always comparing the "amazing transformation" to a caterpillar bursting into a butterfly or a bud blossoming into a flower . . . as if butterflies and flowers had to deal with divorced parents or trying on new bathing suits.

I wanted nothing to do with growing up. I would

be perfectly fine living as a caterpillar in a cocoon, or a closed bud, for the rest of my life.

"Remember, it doesn't usually happen all at once," Mo continued. "You should see spotting first."

"Gross." I groaned. "Can you keep it down? The whole restaurant can hear you."

She scanned the nearly empty patio. "You mean those two people sitting over in the corner? They aren't listening to us."

My dad, Mo's ex-husband, sometimes calls her a bulldozer, because she plows over everything in her path to pave her own wide road. I know it isn't as if she purposely talks too loudly or sits too close or offends strangers with her public comments, but I wish there was a library book she could read on becoming a normal mother.

"I really don't want to talk about it," I said through clenched teeth, "especially not here."

"For crying out loud," said Mo, after diving into the basket of complementary pita chips and stuffing several into her mouth, "it's the most natural thing in the world!"

The thought of blood seeping uncontrollably from my body every month for the next 35 to 40 years sounded like the most *unnatural* thing in the world. It seemed only fair that I got a choice in all of this, or at the very least, a few more years to be a kid. I had just turned twelve less than a month ago.

Mo reached over and squeezed my hand. I tried to pull away, but she held tighter.

"I want you to know, Agnes, that the conversation is always open. You'll experience a lot of changes and there's nothing you can't ask me. Got it?"

Agnes. That's what my father allowed my bulldozing mother to name me.

My older sister and I were named after Mo's grandmothers: Nana Vivian and Granny Agnes. According to Mo, my sister couldn't say her name, Vivian, when she was little and called herself "Viva," which basically means *live it up!* Of course, everyone thought that was adorable, so Viva stuck. And it fits her perfectly. Viva has always been wild and brave, as if nothing scares her.

Seven years after my sister's arrival I was born. But I talked early and in full sentences, which meant I pronounced my name flawlessly. So, unfortunately for me, *Agnes* stuck. A couple of years ago my best friend, Megan, tried calling me Aggie, but that sounded even worse, like something you'd call an old donkey.

I wished more than anything I had a pretty name like Isabelle or Sophia or Chloe . . . but I know I'm nothing like those names.

"Got it, geez, Mo." I groaned louder this time. "Can we please change the subject?"

"You're right," she said just as the server reappeared with our orders. Mo attacked her wrap with an extra-large bite. Chunks of chicken fell onto her plate.

"The reason I wanted to have this mother-daughter day," she continued between chomps, "is to kick off our awesome summer plans."

I took a sip of my smoothie. "In case you forgot, I already have my own awesome plans."

For once, I wouldn't be spending endless hours at the boring town-sponsored day camp. This summer, Megan and I were finally old enough to volunteer at the humane society, which was a dream come true, especially for me. I love animals, but Mo is allergic to everything, so Viva and I have never been allowed to have pets, not even a gerbil.

"Well, things are about to get even more awesome," said Mo, as she wiped her chin with her napkin and grinned. "So you need to pack up your entire bedroom by Tuesday."

Chapter 2

"What? Why?" I blurted, no longer concerned about the quiet couple in the corner. "Are we moving?"

"Not permanently," said Mo, as she sucked the dregs of her iced tea through the straw. "Just through August. I've already found a renter for the house while we spend a glorious summer in the *Sunflower State*."

She swept her arm toward a rose bush as if we'd already arrived.

"The what state?"

"Kansas! Where the earth is flat and the sky is wide, and sunflowers thrive. You can practically live on the seeds—not to mention, the blossoms are spectacular. Nothing like a field filled with sunflowers."

"Why Kansas?" I asked.

"It just so happens Richard received a significant grant to paint outdoor murals at the Topeka Museum of Recycled Art. I am so proud of him, putting himself out there, I could burst!"

My mother often makes huge, random decisions without considering how those decisions will affect other people. So even though I was upset to hear this news for the first time, nothing Mo did shocked me anymore. Especially since the divorce.

My family fell apart a year ago when Mo and Dad told Viva and me that they could no longer live together. They had always argued a lot, but then suddenly they stopped fighting and began speaking calmly to each other, like they were strangers. That's when I knew something was really wrong.

Mo eventually explained that she and my father were simply different peas meant to live in separate pods. You would think two adults could figure that out before they got married and had kids.

My father, Timothy Moon, is a professional cellist who teaches at Prelude Conservatory, a special college for musicians. Right after my parents told us they were splitting up, Dad and his cello moved into one of the faculty apartments at the school, which is about an hour north, in the town of Bittersweet.

According to the custody agreement, Viva and I were supposed to stay at Dad's place two weekends a month. But then Viva turned eighteen and claimed she no longer had to do anything our parents told her to do. A few months later, after her first semester at the state university in Burlington, she quit college to work on a soybean farm. And now none of us see her.

So I'm the only one who visits Dad.

He doesn't even own a real bed, only a lumpy pull-out couch and a reclining chair that he sleeps in whenever I stay over. And since he doesn't have any cooking facilities, other than a small fridge and a microwave, everything we eat in his apartment is either pre-packaged or take-out food. But staying with him is still better than being at home.

Almost immediately after my father left us, Mo started dating, which shocked me. I assumed she was chatting it up with customers at Fred's Meds, where she works as a pharmacist, and that maybe one of the elderly widowers had asked her out.

But then one day, Mo left her laptop open and there it was: the profile of a 47-year-old real estate agent (and amateur magician). *A dating site.* Besides being disgusted, I was stunned that she'd actually figured out how to use it. She still has trouble texting a coherent message.

Mo met a variety of men before settling on Richard, *the mumbler*, a painfully quiet artist.

We happen to have an old wooden shed in our backyard, where my dad used to store all our bicycles. But within weeks, Mo gave the shed to Richard to use as a painting studio. Soon after, he got full access to our tiny two-bedroom house. So did his six-year-old son, George, who stays with him—and now us—on Wednesdays and Saturdays. It felt as if I'd lost my family, my privacy, and my body all in one year. And now we were moving?

Our waiter arrived with the check and, after asking for a container to take home a leftover pickle and five sweet potato fries, Mo handed him a credit card.

"But Kansas sounds hot," I said. "And annoying and boring."

"Of course Kansas isn't boring—it's chock full of things to do and see! We'll have tons of adventures. And you can thank Richard for that."

I had yet to come across one reason to thank Richard. As far as I was concerned, he and his strange kid were unwelcome guests in my life and our already crowded house.

Mo signed the receipt, then insisted we take a loop through the center of town on our way back to the car.

x x x

The potential for humiliation worried me whenever I walked in public with my mother, so I kept my gaze glued to the ground.

"Well, I can't go with you," I said, staring down as I followed her. "I already signed up at the humane society."

"Don't you think they have stray animals in the Midwest?"

"Of course, but I promised Megan."

"I'll call her mother and explain. Maybe Megan can fly out for a visit."

I glanced around to make sure it was safe to look up. We were standing in front of a pottery shop.

"This doesn't make any sense, Mo. Why can't Richard go alone?"

"Alone? Don't you think he deserves to have our support?"

"But what about your job? Have you thought about that?"

Mo cupped her hands around her eyes and studied a display of matching coffee mugs. "The drugstore was more than happy to give me a leave of absence. So now we can all move to Topeka for the summer and cheer on Richard in his groundbreaking endeavor."

"Wait. Did you just say *all* of us? Even Viva?"

This trip wouldn't be so horrible if it meant spending time with my sister. Even though Viva lived only a couple hours away, none of us had heard from her since last Thanksgiving, the same week Richard had moved in.

"There's no point in asking Viva," she said as she continued walking. "Your sister still refuses to answer my calls or emails."

My heart sank. I tried not to take Viva's absence personally, but it didn't seem fair that I was forced to deal with the leftovers of our family by myself.

"Then who's *all of us* if Viva isn't going?"

Across the street, a girl flipped her long, silky hair behind her shoulders. It was Lux Lockhart, the new kid at school. Even though she'd moved into town only a month or so ago, the entire sixth grade seemed to be obsessed with her. Apparently, she was rich and used to live somewhere in Europe. Luckily, she didn't seem to notice me.

"Let's see," said Mo, "there's you, Richard, myself, and then Richard's brother may join us for a week or two."

Lux checked her phone, then rushed over to some guy waiting in front of a vegan restaurant and they hurried in together.

"And, of course, little Georgie will be with us."

I whipped around. "*George*? For the whole summer?"

"His mother loves the idea," said Mo as she stopped and pressed her face against the window of a candle shop. "She thinks it would be a fantastic experience for him."

"Of course she thinks it would be a fantastic experience for him, so she can get rid of that brat for three months. There's no way I'm going if he's going."

This was such typical bulldozer behavior from my mother, shoving everyone together in a heap first, and then attempting to smooth over the pile of problems she creates later.

"For crying out loud, Agnes, you can't stay home alone for the summer," said Mo, as I followed her through a door into a clothing shop, "and you can't live in that sardine can at the college with your father for more than a weekend. Besides, this will be good for you and Georgie."

"Are you joking? That kid isn't normal, Mo. He talks in a fake British accent and collects buttons."

"Oh, that'll pass. Georgie is a very bright boy who's having a little difficulty filtering his emotions," said Mo. Then she gazed in a large arc, as if watching a puff of dust float through the air. "Now, where should we start?"

That's when I realized I'd been lured into another sea of swimwear.

"I'm not going to Kansas, Mo, and I'm definitely not trying on any more bathing suits!"

Before she could respond, I escaped from the store and ran all the way back to the car.

Chapter 3

That night was the annual end-of-school sleepover at my best friend Megan's house with our other friends Rachel and Olivia. We'd done it every year since second grade. But this year felt different.

Megan and I hadn't seen each other since last week, which happened sometimes, since we weren't in the same class. So we had a lot to catch up on, starting with Rachel and Olivia, who had been acting strange lately. In fact, I wouldn't be surprised if those two didn't show up at all.

The four of us had met in preschool and had done almost everything together over the years, like softball and girl scouts. But during the last few months, Megan and I had noticed them pulling away, almost as if they were embarrassed to be our friends.

It all started when they both got new phones for

Christmas. Having a smartphone always changes people. For one thing, they check them constantly, as if the online world is the real world. But Rachel and Olivia took it a step further, implying that anyone without a smartphone was somehow beneath them. Including Megan and me. We still had old-fashioned basic phones, which we only used to text each other, or our parents when we needed a ride.

So on top of all that, now I'd have to report Mo's latest plot to ruin my life. Especially since I knew Megan wouldn't volunteer at the Humane Society without me. It occurred to me that maybe I could live with her family for the summer. Megan was an only child and it seemed like her parents would do practically anything she asked.

"Good, you're early," said Megan as I squeezed through her front door lugging my sleeping bag, pillow, and overnight duffel. "Did you remember to bring two bottles of nail polish to swap?"

I laughed. "Like I own nail polish, very funny."

I carried my stuff down the hallway to the game room where they had a pool table and a widescreen TV above the gas fireplace. I loved Megan's house. It was tidy and perfect, the exact opposite of mine.

"Didn't you read the message with the invite?"

"Since when do I need an invite to spend the night at your house? Hey, where are your parents? I have another idea about this summer and—"

"If you'd read it, you'd know we're doing a mani-pedi polish swap," she interrupted, ignoring my question.

"Wait, you're serious?"

She stared at me expectantly without answering.

"Come on, Megan, you're joking, right?" I said as I dropped everything in my favorite sleeping location, between the couch and the wall in the far corner of the room.

Now she bit her lip, and it became uncomfortably clear that she wasn't joking.

"Was this Rachel and Olivia's idea?"

"I guess," she finally admitted, "but everyone does it."

Something weird was going on. Megan never paid attention to what everyone else was doing. That's exactly why I liked her.

Just then I noticed she was wearing a dress, a short sundress. We never wore dresses.

"What's with the outfit?" I asked, and took a closer look at her face and hair. "Are you wearing makeup? And did you get *highlights*?"

Another thing I liked about Megan was her general lack of interest in her appearance, something neither of us had ever cared about. But now she tossed her new streaky waves across her back and grinned as if posing for a selfie.

"Like it?" she squeaked, then covered her mouth and giggled. "My mom took me to her salon this morning for an end-of-the-school-year present. Her stylist, Damien, is phenomenal."

"Your mother let you do that?"

She nodded. "Isn't it great?"

Fortunately, she didn't seem to expect me to respond. I scanned the room still convinced this was some kind of prank. Megan was playing the part of every girl we couldn't stand at school.

"Oh, and guess what?" she said as she reached into her pocket. "Another gift from my parents. I got it a few days ago."

It was a smartphone.

"But I thought your parents said you couldn't have one until high school? Like my parents."

She shrugged as if it was no big deal. "Someone told my mom that everyone in middle school has them, and that I definitely would need one if I was going to, you know, fit in better."

Fitting in wasn't something Megan and I had ever tried to do. How could she have changed so much in one week?

The doorbell rang and she bolted out of the room. I couldn't believe Rachel and Olivia were early too. Now I'd never get a chance to talk with Megan and figure out what was going on with everyone in my life, including her.

"Oh, hey," said a voice.

I turned around and froze.

"Agnes, you know Lux, right? She moved here like a month ago?"

Of course, Megan knew I knew about the new girl. Everyone did. And we had made fun of everyone else falling all over themselves trying to be friends with the new girl.

"Am I early?" asked Lux.

She also wore a little sundress and lip gloss, along with strings of necklaces and crystal earrings shaped like tiny chandeliers. Her long, silky hair draped down across her arms in loose waves.

"Right on time," said Megan, who was grinning so hard I thought her braces would pop out of her mouth. "Olivia and Rachel will be here any minute."

The new girl's eyes drifted between my Kettleboro

Kamp T-shirt and the plastic flip-flops Mo bought for me last summer at the drugstore with her employee discount. Then she dropped down onto the couch and sighed.

Megan rubbed her hands together. I tried to get her attention by sending a silent *Why is she here?* signal, but it was as if she was avoiding me.

"Do you want anything, Lux? A soda? Sparkling cider?" Megan asked.

"Nah," she muttered, like she was killing time in the waiting room of a doctor's office. "I meant to have my stepfather stop at Sparhawks for a latte. I get so sluggish this time of day."

She yawned.

"Yeah, me too," said Megan, chewing on her bottom lip. For a second, I thought she was going to offer to walk all the way to Sparhawks, but then the doorbell rang again.

Suddenly, Lux and I were alone. I didn't know how to talk to a girl like her. Before tonight, I had assumed Megan didn't either. But I had no chance to try. Lux was already curled over her phone, grinning at some post, as if I didn't exist.

Down the hall I heard Olivia and Rachel squeal, *"She's here?"*

They also wore short, flowy dresses, strappy shoes, and an array of accessories. Without even saying hello to me, they piled onto the couch and surrounded Lux like crazed fans. And all four of them clung to their smartphones.

Instantly, the room felt smaller and hotter.

When I was at school, I often felt left out of those tight girl circles, as if I'd been born insignificant and didn't deserve to be in them. But it had never mattered to me much, because I knew I always had these three girls. Especially Megan. Until now.

×××

Megan's parents had gone out to dinner, so Megan ordered pizza on her smartphone and paid with her mom's card, something I'd never seen her do before. After we ate, I leaned against the wall for what felt like an hour, while they swapped polish and painted their nails, gossiped, shared makeup, played endless rounds of *I Never*, took selfies, and posted every moment online.

Just like the rest of the sixth-grade class, all three of them drooled over Lux, who seemed to know everything about surviving middle school, including how to get a boy to like you, as if that was the only reason to go to school.

We also found out that Lux was short for Luxembourg, which, according to her, is the best country in all of Europe because her parents were married there. Even though they split up a few years later and now she has her stepfather's last name. Then she told us that Italy, where she'd lived the longest, was her true home, but that she'd also spent time in France, Brazil, and Russia. And she had an older stepbrother living in Germany, where he used to be a famous professional soccer player.

I was relieved when I heard the electric garage door open.

Now that Megan's parents were back, I knew we would finally do something fun together, like team charades or superhero trivia. And eat whoopee pies. Her family made homemade whoopee pies for every occasion, which was another reason why I loved hanging out with Megan. Not only were her parents amazing and her house huge and uncluttered, her family did the things a happy family was supposed to do together.

But as soon as her mom and dad walked inside, they called out, "Good night!" and disappeared upstairs. They didn't even make eye contact with me.

"Movie time?" said Lux.

Immediately, Megan, Rachel, and Olivia spread out their sleeping bags. Except Lux, who wrapped herself in a down comforter that she'd bought in Iceland. The four of them lined up side by side below the television screen and scrolled through the movie guide, while I slipped into my puppies-and-kittens sleeping bag in the back corner of the room.

"Hey, you've been so quiet," Megan yelled over to me. "What do you want to watch, Agnes?"

She knew exactly why I was quiet. I didn't reply, pretending to be asleep.

"Is she out already?" I heard Lux whisper. "It's only ten o'clock."

"Agnes is having a hard time lately," Megan also whispered. "Her family is kind of a mess these days."

A mess? I couldn't believe Megan was talking about me, and about my personal problems. I knew I complained about my family a lot, but didn't everyone?

"That doesn't explain why she dresses like that," said Olivia. "*You* even said she needs a new wardrobe, Megan."

She did?

"More like a makeover," Rachel added, which made them all giggle.

"She doesn't even wear a bra," said Lux, "and she definitely needs one."

How could she know that? I hated the idea of wearing a bra.

"I don't get what's up with her," said Olivia, "but she'll never survive seventh grade if she doesn't figure it out this summer."

Figure what out? My whole body began to sweat.

"What is she anyway?" asked Lux.

Silence. A long, awkward silence.

Then Megan replied, "What do you mean?"

"She has all those freckles, but she's sort of dark, and her eyes with that hair—I've been all over the world, but I've never seen anyone who looks like her."

"I think her dad is Chinese," said Rachel.

"He's part Korean," Megan corrected her, "but he's American. Her dad was born here. Her mom is white, but she's kind of different looking too."

How could Megan do this to me . . . just to get Lux to like her?

I nearly jumped up and screamed. Instead, I squeezed myself into a very tight ball and forced myself not to cry.

"And what about her weird name?" said Lux. "You guys aren't really friends with *Agnes Moon*, are you?"

Chapter 4

As soon as I knew they were asleep, I gathered my stuff and slipped out the front door. The sky was dark, but the stars lit up the road enough for me to find my way home.

If anyone happened to look out their window, or drive by that late at night, they may have wondered if I was sleepwalking. I didn't care that my clothes were dragging along the curb or that my hair was sticking out in every direction like a pile of spiky dead pine needles. I didn't care about anything or anyone anymore. Because no one cared about me.

I cut through the open field that bordered our yard and crept into our little beige house through the back door, which we never locked. The yellowed linoleum crackled like broken glass as I crossed the kitchen floor. A light in the hallway had been left on. I turned it off before opening the door to my tiny bedroom and crawling into the bottom bunk. I could hear George breathing above me, where he slept every Wednesday and Saturday night. In Viva's old bed.

Even though I was exhausted, I couldn't stop thinking about what they had said, what people must always think when they look at me. *What is she?* Like a bad art project or a failed science experiment or a freak reptile at the zoo.

I hated who I was, what I looked like, how everything had changed for the worse. My body, my family, and now my friends. I would do anything to start over and be someone else. Anyone else. Just not me.

Suddenly there was light. I tried to open my eyes, but it was too bright.

"Will you be joining us for breakfast, ma'am?"

I must have fallen asleep. I sat up and squinted.

"Is that a flashlight? Get it out of my face, George."

The beam vanished, but the morning sun still lit up the room.

"Omelets and organic fruit cups will be served in the main dining area precisely at 9 a.m., ma'am."

He was wearing his official butler jacket, an old black blazer of Richard's with the sleeves rolled up. It practically reached his ankles. A plaid dish towel was draped over his right arm. He pronounced ma'am as *mum*, speaking in his ridiculous fake British accent.

According to Mo, after Richard and his wife got divorced, George started this butler bit every time things got tense between his parents. No one knew if he had read about butlers in a book or seen them in a cartoon, but apparently it helped them all to get past their anger and act kinder toward one another.

I, on the other hand, found his butler act incredibly annoying, and didn't understand why we had to keep encouraging it. But Mo said George's therapist felt it helped him through the healing process, so no one was allowed to even mention it. As if it was normal.

"Go away, George. I'm not hungry."

Just then, Mo leaned through the doorway.

"Hey sleepy head! You're home early. How was Megan's party?"

The cheerful way she spoke caused everything to crash into reality. I dropped back onto my pillow and stuffed my head under the blankets.

"Can everyone please get out of my bedroom and leave me alone?"

"Very well, m' lady." The butler bowed. "Will you be available then for a light luncheon at noon?"

I groaned.

"Sounds like someone didn't get much sleep last night, Georgie," said Mo. "Let's go. Your dad's eggs are getting cold."

I tried to imagine a summer on the other side of the country trapped with these people. At least it would be somewhere far away—not here in Kettleboro where I had no friends. Where everyone thought I was hideous. Maybe we could move to Topeka permanently if Richard got hired by that museum. Mo could probably get a job at a drugstore. But it might include being stuck with George forever. And what about Dad and Viva back here in Vermont?

I let my eyes drift around the room until they landed on *becoming a woman*. The book was on top of my bureau, leaning against a giant pink box of menstrual pads with a glittery bow on top.

Why was my whole life falling apart?

My phone vibrated on my nightstand. I assumed it was Megan texting me from her new smartphone.

There was no way I was talking to her ever again, but it kept vibrating, so I flipped it open just to glance. It was my dad's number. A small photo of a bike appeared on the screen, followed by a text: *What do you think?*

Dad is almost as obsessed with his bicycles as he is with his cello. Mo said it's his way of escaping responsibilities, but I think he likes the way it feels. He once told me that riding as fast as you can down a steep hill is the closest thing to flying.

Cool, I wrote back, relieved to be distracted. *Is it new?*

While I waited for him to reply I checked my messages to see if by any chance Megan had tried to call. Nothing. She probably thought I was still asleep in the corner of her family room.

The bike? No, that's my old hybrid. I mean the house.

I popped up so quickly, my head bumped the bottom springs of the top bunk. The photo showed his bicycle parked against the steps of a yellow porch.

What about the house? I asked.

I'm taking care of it this summer while Julia is away. So maybe you can stay longer than a weekend!

All at once, the world didn't seem completely against me anymore. I called my dad.

"Not a chance, Agnes."

Mo was sitting on the kitchen floor with George, helping him sort through a pile of buttons, as Richard stood in front of the sink filled with soapy water.

"You're not listening," I said. "Dad's living in a house, a big house this summer. Not the dorm. I just talked to him and he said there's more than enough room for me."

Mo's left eyebrow arched into a sideways question mark.

"Who owns this enormous house?"

"His friend, Julia, from the college." Dad had mentioned Julia a few times before, and they seemed to be spending more time together lately. Just last week, Dad had texted me about his latest biking adventure with a photo of the two of them in bike helmets. "She's teaching or doing something somewhere far away this summer, so he's housesitting for her."

"Shall we count the big ones or the little ones first?" asked the butler, butting in and hogging all the attention as usual. "I rather like these wooden buttons."

Mo held onto Richard's leg as she hoisted herself up from the floor. "Why don't you separate them first into all the subgroups, Georgie? I'll be right back."

Richard glanced over his shoulder and mumbled something to Mo. He was wearing his daily uniform, an old T-shirt with some political statement and ripped jeans, both speckled in paint. His stringy silver hair, like always, was pulled back into a pitiful pony tail.

"I know, Richard," Mo replied, "and I appreciate it, but I don't agree."

Mo was the only person who could ever hear the mumbler, which didn't make sense since her idea of a normal conservation was shouting.

She dragged me by the elbow toward the den, as far away as we could get from the kitchen.

"What are you doing?" I said and yanked my arm back. "Why are you making such a big deal out of this?"

"Because this trip means a lot to Richard," said Mo. For once, she kept her voice down.

"Is that what he mumbled to you? That it means a lot to him?"

Mo frowned. "Not exactly, but you know he doesn't like to upset anyone."

"And you do?" I snapped.

"Listen to me, Agnes. This summer will be a wonderful chance for the four of us to bond as a family."

"Except my family includes Dad and Viva, not your freeloading boyfriend and his mutant offspring."

Mo's whole body went rigid as she stuck her thick finger in my face.

"I don't know what's gotten into you lately, Agnes Moon, but you need to shape up, and shape up fast! Richard and Georgie are part of our lives now, and that's not going to change. Got it?"

As a matter of fact, that was exactly the moment when I *got it* . . . when I knew I had to do something drastic to change my life. To change *me*.

There was no way I was staying in this town or going with Mo and her new family to Kansas. I was spending this summer with my father, the only person who cared a sliver about my feelings.

"I didn't want to have to tell you this, because I promised Dad I wouldn't."

She dropped her finger and crinkled her forehead. "Well, it sure sounds like you should, Agnes, so spill it."

I took a deep breath to add dramatic effect. "He's not doing very well," I lied, frowning. "He sounds terrible."

"What are you saying? Is Timothy sick?"

For once, I had her full attention.

"He didn't give me the details, so I'm not sure what it is exactly, but I could tell that he really wants me to come this summer. I think it's partly why he got the housesitting job."

Mo's head dropped. I was surprised how easily these little fibs fell out of my mouth. It actually felt good to twist the truth.

"Well, this changes everything," she said and sighed.

As if on cue, George appeared and yanked on Mo's sleeve.

"Come on, Mo," he said in his non-butler, bratty voice, "I'm done separating all the buttons. I want to count them now."

My mother wrapped her arm around his shoulders and pulled him close.

"Of course, you should be with him, Agnes," she said softly as she patted George. "I don't know why he didn't tell me himself, but I'll call him."

"Call who?" George whined.

I panicked a little. "But you *have to* promise not to tell Dad what I told you, Mo. I'm sure he'll tell you when he's ready to share."

That was one thing Mo respected: therapy talk. The four of us had been in therapy together as a family, and even post-family a few times. Mo was the only one who ever seemed to get anything out of those sessions. But they did come in handy as lessons in persuasion. If you ever wanted to convince my mother of something, speaking in therapy talk worked best.

George blurted, "Tell you what? Share what? Can I have one?"

"It's nothing, Georgie," replied Mo. "Wait for me in the kitchen. I'll be right there."

As he stomped away in his full-length butler blazer, Mo gave me one of her too tight, too long hugs.

"Of course, I'll keep it between us, Agnes." Then she added, "I hope you know you can always trust me."

And there it was. Just like that, I got my way. I couldn't remember the last time that had happened.

Chapter 5

Before I left for Dad's on Tuesday night, Mo forced me to pack everything I owned into cardboard boxes to store in our musty basement all summer. Even though I pointed out the renter would have no need for a miniature bedroom with wobbly bunkbeds, Mom still insisted I clear out every item, down to the last paperclip. Luckily George was spending the day with his mother, so he wasn't around pestering me. But still, I almost didn't finish in time to make the last bus to Bittersweet.

Before I grabbed my duffel bag and raced out the door, Richard startled me with a small pat on my back. He didn't say anything, as usual, but I could tell he was trying to say something. Whatever it was, I didn't want to hear it. I wanted to get away from there as fast as I could.

At the bus station, Mo was too preoccupied with their upcoming trip to make a big deal out of mine.

"Let me know immediately if your father's condition changes," she said. At first I thought she meant the housesitting, but then I remembered my little health fib. "And don't forget to always wash your hands after being in public places, never eat grapes unless they're organic, and call me if you get any spotting."

I couldn't believe she was bringing that up again as her last words to me. "Are you done yet?"

"You have all the contact numbers, right?"

"I have everything, Mo." I pecked her on the cheek and jumped out of our old minivan.

"Can I bring back anything special from the mighty Midwest? Turquoise jewelry? A cropped country top? A cute straw hat?"

"Just take lots of pictures," I said and shut the door. Then I leaned in the window and added as a second thought, "And maybe some of those seeds to grow a few sunflowers."

xxx

After the divorce, my father not only taught college students, he pretty much lived with them too.

His apartment building was meant for young, single teachers who couldn't afford their own off-campus apartments. My father wasn't young, and he wasn't completely on his own if you counted Viva and me. But he was a popular professor and an accomplished cellist, so they made an exception for him.

It always felt awkward to be constantly surrounded by his students, especially those who considered my father to be a musical genius. They stopped him on campus to ask questions and interrupted us when we ate in the dining hall, like he was a celebrity. They rarely noticed I was even there until Dad introduced me.

Technically, my parents had divorced only each other, but in some ways it felt as if they'd divorced Viva and me as well. They never seemed to have the time—or want to make the time—for just us anymore. We constantly had to share them with strangers. So when my dad agreed to let me live with him all summer in a big house away from the college campus, it was a dream come true for me—something I'd thought would never happen again. For almost three months, I would have my father all to myself.

As soon as I spotted him across the bus station, I raced over and hugged him so tightly that tears filled my eyes. Lately I felt like crying all the time, but this felt different. Like tears of relief. Dad kissed the top of my head, then bent over and picked up my duffel bag.

"This is all you need until Labor Day Weekend?" he asked.

I didn't want reminders of my life back in Kettleboro, so I hadn't packed much other than a few changes of clothes. Of course, the giant box of menstrual pads with the bow on top had been left behind as well.

"It's summer!" I said. "Plus, I figured you had shampoo and all that junk."

Dad draped his arm over my shoulders as we walked out into the dark night air. "The house is well stocked," he said and smiled. "I think you'll like it."

We climbed into a fancy green sports car with no back seat, another cool perk of this housesitting deal. Since the divorce, my father hadn't been able to afford a car. He usually borrowed one or got rides when he performed. For the most part, he rode his bicycle everywhere, even in winter if the roads were plowed.

As we drove out of the parking lot, Dad kept glancing over at me.

"What?" I said.

"When did you get so much older, Agnes? It's as if you've changed overnight. I think you're as tall as I am now."

My father is actually shorter than my mother, not something you see that often. But everything about Mo and her personality feels too big to me. My dad is athletic and always on the move, so he's never seemed small—more like compact and efficient.

"So what are we going to do for the next three months?" I asked, preferring not to talk about the ways my body had changed.

"It's your summer vacation. What do you feel like doing?"

I was so focused on putting everything behind me, I hadn't thought that far ahead. "I'm up for anything," I said, "even hiking in the woods or watching those boring documentaries you like."

Dad drove slowly through the center of Bittersweet, past the sloping lawn in front of the college. The formal stone buildings, illuminated by spotlights, looked bigger at night. I felt as if we were driving through a long tunnel where a new beginning awaited us at the other end.

"Listen, Agnes," said Dad as we turned off Main Street and onto an unfamiliar road, "I love that you want to spend time with me. And I'm really thrilled you're here. But I'm afraid I have to lock myself in the second-floor office and work all day. At least for the next six or seven weeks."

"What do you mean?" My father hardly ever stayed indoors other than to practice. "Are you getting ready for a big concert?"

I used to enjoy listening to my dad play the cello, even when he practiced endless hours in our little living room, and Mo forced Viva and me to keep quiet or stay outside. But ever since the divorce, it was as if his cello had morphed into the enemy, like a swamp creature that invaded our family and lured my dad away from us.

"Actually, I'm not performing at all this summer," he replied. "I'm taking some time off to finish my PhD."

It turned out the real reason Dad was living away from campus and housesitting was to write his dissertation. That's a very long report, as long as a book, which you have to write if you want to get a PhD and become a doctor of something. For my dad, it was a Doctor of Music Composition, which meant he would be an expert in writing orchestral pieces, featuring his beloved cello, of course.

As far as I could tell, my father had been working on graduate degrees his entire life, but I assumed it was something all professional musicians did. Although I knew it was another detail about Dad that upset Mo, who claimed he could never finish anything.

"Why do you have to write another paper?" I asked. "You already teach at a college and play in their orchestra."

"Lots of reasons," he said, shifting the clutch to climb a steep hill, "but most importantly, once I get my PhD I'll make more money, so I can buy my own car and live in a nicer place, and you can visit more often."

That sounded good in the long term, but disastrous for my summer plans. I didn't know anyone in Bittersweet, and there was nothing to do out here in farm country. I'd assumed Dad would spend a lot of time with me, because he never taught classes during the summer. It hadn't occurred to me he would be busy with something other than practicing his cello and riding his bike.

But as soon as I reminded myself of all the horrible things the girls had whispered about me, especially Megan—or the thought of spending months in

Topeka with the miniature butler—I knew I wanted to be here more than anywhere else.

"I don't mind," I said, and then fibbed, "I have stuff I'm working on too."

"Good," he replied and sighed. "I'm glad to hear that. And you can have friends, like Megan, visit if you want. The house has three bedrooms and four bathrooms!"

I didn't want to think about Megan, and definitely didn't want to explain the real reason why I wouldn't be inviting her. So I said the first thing that popped into my head. "Her family's kind of a mess right now. I think her parents are probably getting divorced."

"Daniel and Annie are splitting up?" said Dad. "Wow, never would have guessed. Those two seem so close. How's Megan doing?"

It was funny. I didn't even have to think about my version of the facts. They instantly appeared in my head as if they'd really happened.

"Not so great. I feel like I need to take a break from her this summer and let her sort it all out."

Dad looked at me, his eyebrows scrunched in concern. "But don't you think she needs you now more than ever?"

I shook my head. "She's made it pretty clear she doesn't need me at all."

That part was true, and it hurt. So I decided to stick with the made-up, painless version.

"By the way, Megan made me promise not to tell anyone," I fibbed some more, "so I haven't told Mo any of this. You won't tell anyone, will you?"

He reached over and covered my hand. "You can trust me, Agnes. I'm sorry Megan is having a hard time, but I won't tell a soul."

Chapter 6

The best news of all was, along with a gigantic house and a cool sports car all to ourselves for the entire summer, we were taking care of a dog! An adorable, shaggy little dog with pointy ears and scruffy fur.

"Why didn't you tell me?" I said as I dropped to the floor and gathered Tutu into my arms.

"I thought it would be a fun surprise. I know how much you like dogs."

"I *love* dogs. I even had a volunteer job lined up at the—" I caught myself and stopped. I didn't want to think about how the summer was supposed to be. That was behind me now.

"At the where?" he asked, as he put away the groceries he'd bought before picking me up at the bus station.

I pretended not to hear and changed the subject. "So how old is Tutu?"

"She's twelve years old, like you," he smiled. "Young for humans, old for dogs."

Tutu rolled onto her back for a belly rub.

"Can she sleep with me?"

Dad folded up his canvas shopping bags and tucked them in a cabinet. I had been here only a few minutes and already this place felt like home.

"I'm sure she would if she could. But the bedrooms are on the second floor and she has to be carried up the stairs. Arthritis in her hips. Probably best if she sleeps on her comfy bed in the back hall."

I stood up and Tutu copied me. "Where's the bathroom?"

"Three upstairs and one through that door behind the family room," he replied as he pointed at the far corner.

Since I'd never lived in a house with more than one bathroom, I had a hard time choosing. "Which one's the best?" I asked.

"Hard to say—they all have a view of the river."

"We're close to a river too?"

Dad grinned. "I knew you'd like it here."

The next morning I sprang out of bed, threw back the curtains, and opened the window. Ribbons of sunshine and the sound of rushing water filled the room. In the distance, just beyond a meadow of wildflowers, the river sparkled. No other houses in sight, nothing but soft green fields and tall trees.

It was hard to believe how miserable I had been only a couple of days ago, and now I was happier than I'd been in my entire life. Having so much space to myself felt better than I'd ever imagined. For three months, I wouldn't have to share a bedroom, a bathroom, a pet, or even my dad with another person.

After washing up, I slipped a black tank top over my head and pulled on denim shorts. An antique, full-length mirror hung on a stand in the corner by the bureau. I forced myself to take a look. The curves were starting to feel familiar, even though I still didn't like them.

"Morning, everyone," I sang as I bounded down the stairs.

Tutu was waiting for me at the bottom step, wagging her stubby tail. Dad stood by the kitchen counter, dressed in bike pants and a fluorescent yellow shirt. "How'd you sleep?"

"Great! Where were you?"

"Took my early morning ride." He clapped his hands together and checked his watch. "Now it's time to work! How about we meet back here for dinner at seven?"

"I guess," I said and looked down at Tutu. "What about her?"

"She's had her breakfast and I let her out already, but she loves walks and will follow you as long as you have a couple of dog biscuits in your pocket. Just bring a leash in case you need it."

"Where am I supposed to walk her?"

"Anywhere you want, but don't overdo it—she's getting on in years."

Dad bent down to give Tutu a quick pat, kissed the top of my head, then jogged up the stairs. "I'll be up in the office if you need me, Agnes, but only if it's an emergency. After seven, I'm all yours."

This was one of the main differences between Mo and my dad. He believed children should have as little direction and supervision as possible to learn through experience and make their own decisions. Mo, on the other hand, believed that she was put on the earth to tell everyone what to do and how to do it.

Which was why as soon as I turned my phone on, I saw about a dozen texts from Mo. I scrolled quickly through the messages, sighing, until suddenly I saw Megan's name. Without thinking, I clicked on her message: *Is it true? You're gone all summer??*

Instead of feeling angry, now I felt guilty, as if I had been caught doing something I shouldn't. I had to remind myself that it was Megan who had betrayed me, not the other way around.

I powered the phone off, vowing to check it as little as possible while I was here. When Viva and I were younger, Mo had a million rules to limit our screen time, so really, she should be pleased that I wasn't answering all her texts right away.

After eating a bowl of cereal, I grabbed some dog biscuits and the leash. But Tutu was already curled up on her bed in the back hall, sound asleep. It looked like I would have to explore this new world all by myself.

When I'd arrived the night before, it had been so dark I could barely find my way from the car to the front porch. Now, outside in the daylight, I could see the house was painted buttery yellow with cream trim. An enormous tree with a double trunk shaded the front yard, and the green sports car was parked in front of an old red barn.

Not one car passed me as I strolled up the road along the river, hearing only the loud flow of water. In the distance I saw a little stone bridge. Something drew me toward it, so I walked down to see what was on the other side.

As I paused in the middle of the bridge and leaned over the railing, a faint rainbow appeared in the water between two rocks. If I moved my head too far one way or the other, it vanished, so I stared directly at it for as long as I could.

All at once, it occurred to me it didn't matter if I stood there in that spot the whole day. I had all the time in the world with nothing I had to do, and no one who needed me or who would even look for me. At least not until dinnertime. And that's how it would be for the entire summer.

When I really thought about that endless stream of time all alone, my heart began to pound. But then I glanced up the river and saw our beautiful yellow house through the tall leafy trees. I thought about Dad upstairs in the office and Tutu sleeping on her bed, and my worries faded.

It was already hot and the air was muggy. I found a scrunchie in my pocket and twisted my thick hair into a bun before I continued exploring. On the other side of the bridge I was surprised to discover I had entered a different town. A sign, partially hidden by bushes, read:

Welcome to
RENEW, VERMONT
Settled in 1782

Not far up the road on the left was a general store with a sign that said *Birdie's*. Bundles of firewood were stacked along the front of the building. As I pushed open the door, a string of bells jangled on the other side.

"Hi there," an older girl called from behind the counter.

The store seemed to be empty except for this girl. She looked about Viva's age and had a round face, long dark hair parted down the middle, and thick-rimmed glasses.

"Looking for anything in particular?" she asked as she pushed her glasses against the top of her nose and blinked in a fluttery way.

"Not really," I said. "I got here last night, so I'm just wandering around."

She dropped forward onto her elbows, between the old-fashioned cash register and a basket of peppermint candies. "Got in from where?"

I hesitated. I had never met this girl before, and we didn't know each other or any of the same people. Besides, the truth was too depressing to think about.

"Topeka," I replied, which felt surprisingly good to say.

"Is that over in Maine? My whole family comes from—"

"No, it's in Kansas."

The girl straightened her back. "Wow, that's far."

I smiled, pleased with my choice.

"You don't sound like you're from somewhere like Kansas."

I hadn't thought of that. I wondered what someone from Kansas sounded like. "We move around and travel a lot," I lied a little more, "so I don't have an accent."

"You're lucky. I never get to go anywhere," she said. "What's your name?"

This time I didn't hesitate, not for a second. "Chloe."

She tilted her head. "That's a cool name. You look like a Chloe."

No one had ever said those words to me.

"My name's Estelle. Isn't that awful?"

I didn't think Estelle was nearly as bad as Agnes, but I couldn't tell her that. "It's not awful."

"No one calls me that anyway. I've always been Stella, which is a little better."

She had one of those open smiles that immediately made me trust her without even knowing her.

"Do you want some cider donuts, Chloe?" asked Stella. "I made them myself. You can take some home."

She moved down along the wooden counter and lifted the top of a glass jar.

"They look really good, but I didn't bring any money."

She selected a half-dozen sugary donuts with a pair of wooden tongs and carefully placed them into a white paper bag. "You can have them. Consider it a *Welcome to Renew* gift! We always end up with leftovers at the end of the day anyway. We used to take them home, but then we ate way too many for our own good," she said and laughed.

I glanced around the store but didn't see or hear anyone else. I wondered who she meant by *we*.

"Are you some kind of prima ballerina, Chloe?"

"A–sorry?" I stammered, confused.

She pointed at my head. "The bun? The black tank top. You've got the whole dancer vibe going on."

I touched the back of my neck and smiled. "I've taken some ballet classes and jazz," I fibbed—so easily! "But it's been a while. I've been so busy."

"Busy with what?"

"Acting mostly."

I couldn't believe I'd said that. It was as if someone else was talking for me. Even my voice sounded different, more confident.

But Stella believed me. I could tell, because her mouth dropped open and her wide eyes doubled in size behind her thick glasses. "That's incredible! Have I seen you in a movie or anything?"

I began to sweat a little. "I meant theater, that kind of acting." Her face dropped in disappointment, so I added, "But I've been in a couple commercials."

She smiled again. "Like what?"

"Nothing around here," I replied quickly, "just local ads for clothes and stuff in Topeka. No big deal."

A rush of pure excitement surged through my

body. I couldn't understand why making this stuff up felt so great.

"How long have you been acting?"

"Since I was around four, so about ten years ago."

That made me fourteen years old, two years older than I was. I wasn't sure Stella would buy it until she asked, "So you're in high school?"

"Not yet," I said less convincingly. "This fall."

I didn't know how much longer I could keep up with these questions. I tried to think of some way to direct the conversation away from me for a minute so that I could catch my breath. I glanced out the large picture window at the front of the store. Across the street was a farm stand, where a boy was unloading vegetables from a wheelbarrow. He looked about my age, but it was hard to tell from this distance.

"Do you know that kid?" I asked.

"Not really. He moved here last winter. He lives with Harriet Hooper, who owns the farm up the dirt road."

I moved closer to the window. Something about the way the boy lifted the crates made him seem years older than he appeared. I turned back to Stella. "What grade is he in?"

"Who knows? He doesn't go to the local school. He's been inside the store only a couple of times, but I can't get him to talk. I offered him free donuts too, but he turned away and said nothing. Not a *thank you* or even just a *no*. It's like he's lost his voice."

The way she said it sent a chill up my spine.

"Can't really blame him though," Stella continued. "I suspect he's an orphan."

"You mean—his parents are dead?"

She nodded and frowned. "That's what I heard. According to Harriet, he's some relative who's come to visit for a while. But she always changes the subject as soon as anyone asks more." She shrugged. "But I figure whatever happened to him has to be terrible if he can't even talk."

All of a sudden, my problems seemed so small compared to that kid's life. Maybe my family was a mess, but at least everyone was still alive. I watched him through the window as he continued to organize the farm stand. He wore a plain shirt and jeans, and his red hair made his skin appear extra pale.

The boy seemed to be done with what he was doing. He took a step back and one last look at the stand. That's when I noticed the words *Fly Back Farm* painted in sky blue letters above the little roof.

He tossed a few crates in the wheelbarrow, then turned around and stared at the general store like he was looking directly at me. After a couple of seconds, he turned away and pushed the wheelbarrow down the dirt road. I leaned against the window and watched him until he disappeared around the bend.

Chapter 7

That evening, I helped Dad make veggie lasagna for dinner in the enormous kitchen, which was so much fun but, at the same time, really strange. For as long as I could remember, Mo had been the one to make dinner at our house, and since Dad had been living on campus all year, I hadn't known he could cook a whole meal.

We sang old songs and told silly jokes as I chopped red peppers and Dad grated the cheese. And a wave of happiness washed over me. This was exactly how I wanted my life to be. Living in a big, comfortable house with an adorable dog and having my dad all to myself.

We ate outside on the patio, taking in the view. When he asked what I'd done during the day, I said I'd gone exploring on my own and had eventually come back to the house to hang out with Tutu, which was basically true. Then I remembered Stella's bag of cider donuts and brought them out on a plate for dessert. As soon as I took a bite, I thought of the boy and asked Dad if he knew the owner of Fly Back Farm.

"I really don't know anyone outside the school, but these donuts are delicious," he said as he took a second one. "Did you get them at that farm?"

"No, at a store."

The evening air was cool as the sun set behind the trees. In the distance I could see a corner of the stone bridge from where we were sitting. I wanted to tell Dad the sad story Stella had told me about the boy, but I stopped myself, realizing he might ask me more and somehow find out about the fibs.

"Is that the general store over in Renew? I should check it out. Do they make other food?"

"I don't know," I muttered, "I don't think so."

Pretending to be Chloe from Kansas—who acted, danced, and made commercials—had felt incredible. Better than I ever remember feeling about myself. But I realized if I wanted Chloe to continue, I would have to keep my two worlds separate, as if the other side didn't exist.

"It was really fun making dinner together," I said and stood up. "Should we do that again tomorrow?"

"I'd love to, but I'll have to take a rain check. Important department meeting, so I'll be late. I'll get some take-out on the way home." Dad picked up a third donut and broke it in half. "Thanks for dessert!"

×××

Tutu was wide awake the next morning. By the time Dad and I finished breakfast, she'd stationed herself at the back door, wagging her crooked little tail. After Dad headed upstairs to work, I stuffed the leash and a couple dog biscuits in my pockets and we took off for the bridge. I knew exactly where I wanted to go.

Tutu took her time sniffing everything as we walked along the road beneath the overcast sky. The bridge was slippery as we crossed. Mist, like fallen clouds, hovered over the river. We passed through the pale fog and, all at once, the sun shone on the other side.

As soon as I passed the *Welcome to Renew* sign, my heart beat a little faster. All the times Mo had babbled on and on about blossoming and transform-ing, I had no idea what that might feel like . . . until now. It had nothing to do with that *becoming a woman* book; it was about becoming the real me.

I'd remembered to grab a scrunchie before I left the house, and now I removed it from my wrist and used it to twist my hair into a bun like a ballerina. And just like that, I left Agnes on the other side of the bridge and became Chloe.

When I peered in the window at the general store, I didn't see Stella. Someone else was behind the counter today. An older woman with short white hair was leaning against the cash register and reading a book. So I crossed the street with Tutu and took a look at the farm stand. Square wooden crates filled with vegetables lined the shelves. And buckets of cut flowers and dark red strawberries in small cardboard containers covered a table to the left. A poster labeled with the words *Honor System* listed prices and instructions about depositing money in a cash box.

Part of me had hoped to run into the boy, but I wasn't sure what I would say to him if I did. Especially if he wasn't able to say anything back. I couldn't imagine what it felt like to be so sad that you could no longer talk, but maybe that was why I was intrigued by him. In an odd way, I sort of knew how he felt. Or at least I thought I did.

I decided to wander down the dirt road toward the farm and beyond the bend, where I had watched him disappear the day before. For a second, I thought I heard cello music playing in the distance. Even though Dad was taking the summer off from performing, I knew he would still practice a few times a week. But it didn't seem possible for me to hear his cello from this far away. I paused under the shade of the trees to listen, but the air was quiet now. Most likely it had been the sound of the river rushing nearby.

The sun was growing hot and Tutu began to lag behind. I remembered what Dad had said, that she was old and I shouldn't overdo it. Just as I bent over to pick her up, she growled at something.

At first I saw only a large animal's nose pushing through a tall bush. Then the next thing I knew a horse stepped out into the road and turned directly toward us.

She was silver with black spots and a white mane. And completely bare, as if she didn't belong to anyone. Tutu stopped growling and wagged her tail. The horse strolled over to us and pressed her nose against my shoulder. I reached up and stroked her neck, even though I'd never been this close to a horse. It was a wonderful feeling, as if Chloe knew exactly what to do.

A sharp whistle pierced the air. Up ahead, the boy from the farm stand stood under a tall tree at a fork in the road. The horse pulled away and trotted toward him, as if she had been searching for him all along. The boy seemed to ignore me as he stretched his arms toward the horse and hugged her. Then he peered around her wide silver body and stared at me as he stroked her mane.

"Hi," I called out and waved.

Tutu jumped up against the back of my legs and whimpered, asking to be carried. By the time I gathered her in my arms and glanced back, the horse and the boy were gone.

Chapter 8

After lunch, as I placed my dishes in the dishwasher, Dad rushed down the stairs announcing he was late for the important meeting and that he would pick up dinner on his way home. The screen door closed behind him and, soon after, I heard the green sports car drive away.

It occurred to me I had the whole house to myself, so I decided to snoop around and see what I could learn about Julia. Considering how much time my dad had been spending with her, I figured I should probably know a little bit about her.

She didn't seem to keep many personal items around the house, other than some jewelry I found in one of the drawers in the downstairs bathroom. Upstairs, I peeked in the office where Dad was working on his dissertation. But there was nothing in there other than a desk covered in papers, pens, and an old computer monitor.

And Dad's cello case.

It was leaning against the wall in the corner of the room behind the door. I went over and stood in front of it, remembering a time when it had been taller than I was. I unbuckled the latches, then slowly opened the cover and stared at the instrument inside.

Ever since the divorce, I'd avoided the cello whenever I saw it in Dad's cramped apartment. I'd blamed it for everything that had gone wrong in our family. But now, as I stood staring at it for the first time in a long time, I knew it was more than blame. I was jealous of that beautiful, shining instrument. As if it was the perfect child, the child Dad had chosen over Viva and me.

I shut the cover and buckled the case quickly, determined to ignore it for good. Then I continued down the hall, passing my bedroom and another empty guest room, until I reached the last bedroom, where Dad slept.

Unlike the rest of the house, this room was overflowing with stuff. The bureau drawers and both closets were filled with women's clothing and a few of Dad's things. A collection of female figurines from other countries was displayed on top of a bookcase, along with unusual artwork hung all over the walls. This was obviously Julia's bedroom. It seemed weird that Dad would sleep in here when he could have the other guest room all to himself.

Near the bottom of the bookcase, I found a photo album. Even though I had never met Julia on any of my weekend visits, I recognized her right away from the photos Dad had texted to me. Everything about her seemed perky: her nose, her chin, her teeth, even her flipped-up blond hair. But she didn't look perky in a fake way, more like a person with a lot of energy.

It was difficult to tell if any of the people in the pictures were her family members or just friends. Some of the photos had children in them, but they were always standing closer to other people, like they didn't belong to her. My dad was nowhere to be found in the album, which was a relief.

I glanced around the cluttered room and saw a few more photos, framed pictures on the bureau near the bed. I was surprised to see a few photographs of Julia and Dad were placed prominently in front. In the largest one, they were sitting next to each other on a giant rock. The view of brown, bare hills that stretched behind them didn't look anything like

Vermont. For a second, I worried they had taken a trip together, but I knew that wasn't possible since Dad always complained about money.

Behind those pictures, I was even more surprised to see a small framed photo of Dad with Viva and me, which I recognized right away because it used to be in our house. The photo had been taken when I was still a baby and Viva was around seven or eight. Both of us are sitting on Dad's lap in our pajamas, surrounded by Christmas stockings and gifts.

And then an even smaller framed photo was hiding behind some books in the corner. It was an old black and white wedding picture of my grandparents, Jin-ho and Elsa Moon, who both died before my parents were married. My dad's father grew up in Korea and his mom was from Sweden. They met in Boston where Dad, their only child, was born. But that was pretty much all I knew about them. Dad always said his parents rarely talked about their earlier lives overseas, and didn't teach him their native languages, because they didn't want him to feel different. As if that were possible.

The weather on their wedding day looked hazy as they stood under a giant willow tree in a park. My grandmother, Elsa, was wearing a lace dress and holding a bouquet of flowers. She was much wider than Jin-ho, who had a big grin on his face. I tried to imagine my father as the son of these two people I'd never met, but I couldn't. They were as distant to me as the moon in the sky.

I took one last look around, with a feeling I couldn't name. Even though this bedroom obviously belonged to Julia, it clearly held some of my dad's memories too—but memories that only barely included me.

✕✕✕

After investigating the entire house, I went outside to poke around the barn. When I slid open the heavy wooden door, a puff of musty air blew past me. It was dark inside, until I pulled a light cord dangling from a rafter. The barn was filled with the usual tools and gardening supplies you'd expect to find, but there were also enough bicycles to open a used bike shop. Now it made sense that my dad and Julia had become such good friends.

When Dad still lived with us in Kettleboro, he always had a bunch of old and broken bikes stored in the backyard shed, because he enjoyed repairing them. Once they were fixed, he never sold them. He gave them away to anyone who wanted a bike.

Years ago, Dad, Viva, and I used to ride together all the time. Then Viva stopped joining us when she was in high school, so it was just Dad and me. But after he left us, I didn't feel like riding anymore.

As soon as Richard moved in and changed the shed to a painting studio, Mo sold the leftover bicycles in a yard sale, including mine. I was at Dad's that weekend and was furious when I got home. Mo claimed Viva and I had lost interest in riding, and that she had given Dad enough time to pick up his extra bikes.

But losing all the bicycles at once, even if no one used them, reminded me that the divorce was final, and that I had lost my family forever. So, in a way, discovering these bikes in the barn seemed like a sign. Maybe our old life hadn't been erased after all. Maybe I'd found it again here in Bittersweet.

Dad had said I could use anything in the house, and I assumed that included stuff in the barn. Most of the bicycles were hybrids, but a blue road bike just my size was leaning against a far corner. It even had a little pouch attached to the back of the seat, big enough to hold my phone or a water bottle.

I found a few helmets on a dusty shelf and picked one that fit me pretty well. A pump was hanging from a hook on the wall, so I gave both tires some air, then rolled the bike out into the driveway and shut the barn door behind me. As I swung my leg over the seat and pedaled down the road, I instantly remembered why I used to love riding so much— that rush of self-propelled freedom you only get on a bike.

Before I knew it, I was on the other side of the bridge parked in front of the store. This time, when I peered through the front window, I saw Stella behind the cash register talking to a customer. A little boy, about two years old, sat on the counter between them. I leaned my bike against the building, took off my helmet, and twisted my hair into a bun. Then I strolled inside pretending I needed to buy something.

"Chloe! You're back."

Being called Chloe felt so good, as if I was meant to be Chloe.

"Come on over and meet my grammy. I've already told her all about you."

As soon as the woman turned, I saw it was the older lady who had been working there earlier that morning. She had Stella's wide face and friendly smile, and even the same thick glasses.

"Pleasure to meet you, Chloe. Stella hasn't stopped talking about you since you walked in the store yesterday." She put her hand out for me to shake, but I wasn't used to shaking people's hands. It felt like something only grown-ups did.

"Hello, Mrs.—?"

"Call me Birdie! Everyone else does."

"Like the name of the store?"

"That's right. My folks opened it sixty-five years ago and named it after me."

The little boy was mesmerized by the cell phone in his hand. I wondered if Stella was babysitting him.

"Chloe's from Kansas and she's an actress," Stella volunteered.

As soon as she said that, I tensed a little. I wouldn't be able to tell them much about the Sunflower State if they asked. "I've only lived there for a couple years," I said. "My family moves around a lot."

"I don't believe I've ever met anyone from Kansas," said her grandmother. "What brings you to our neck of the woods?"

"Yeah," said Stella, "you never did tell me why you're here or for how long."

The little boy pushed a button that made an explosion sound, and then he squealed.

"My parents rented a house for the summer. My dad, mom, my older sister, and me." The words flowed so smoothly, as if they were true.

"Why all the way from Kansas just for the summer?" asked Birdie. "Escaping those tornadoes we always hear about?"

The explanations came so easily, like someone else was saying them. "My mother's a clothes designer. She's part of a big fashion show that's coming up."

Birdie looked confused.

"A fashion show? Around here?"

"Well, not here exactly," I said. "A few towns over."

"That's so cool," said Stella. "What about your father? Is he in the fashion biz too?"

"He's a bank president," I said without hesitation, because it sounded like a rich person's job. And in my perfect world, Dad would be rich and not have to worry about money all the time.

Birdie laughed. "Since when does a bank president get to take off a whole summer?"

This wasn't going as well with an adult as it had with Stella. Luckily, the little boy kicked his feet in the air and giggled, so I took the opportunity to change the subject. "Who's your cute friend?"

Stella wrapped her arms around him, then glanced at Birdie before answering. "This trouble-maker's my nephew."

Her nephew? He looked nothing like Stella. Probably the same way I look nothing like anyone in my family.

"Meet my first great-grandchild," added Birdie, then tugged on his foot. "Be a gentleman, Wyatt, and say hello."

The cell phone had all of his attention.

"Someone's tired," said Stella. "Time for a nap, little man?"

Wyatt whined and shook his head hard. But as soon as Stella lifted him, he melted into her shoulder.

"Thanks for stopping by, Chloe," she whispered. "And bring your sister next time. I'd really love to meet her."

Chapter 9

As I coasted down the dirt road beyond the farm stand, I worried about my collection of little fibs. Most of my exaggerations were easy enough to cover up, but what excuse could I make for a nonexistent sister? Of course, I *did* have a sister, but she wasn't about to show up anytime soon.

Thinking about Viva, about how much I missed her, made my stomach ache the way it does right before I cry. I couldn't figure out what I had done to make her abandon me. I knew it was more about her anger at Mo and the annoying Richard situation. But if I had been the one who had gone off to plant soybeans, I still would have called and texted her all the time, and even visited, no matter how mad I was at Mo.

Suddenly, I realized I was allowing Agnes's crummy life to creep across the bridge and invade

Chloe's world. I needed to put an end to it or this would never work. I shouldn't have been sloppy and used my exact family. Maybe it happened because they weren't my exact family anymore. I didn't know who my family was.

I came to the same fork in the road where I had seen the boy with the horse. A small sign was nailed to the tall tree:

FLY BACK FARM
Wing Repairs

As I stared at the words, trying to figure out what that meant, someone asked, "May I help you?"

I jumped off the bike. "Who said that?"

A branch rustled and I spun around. The boy was just a few feet away.

"You can talk?" I blurted.

He smiled. "Of course I can talk."

His voice was deep, but soft. Standing this close to him, I could see his red hair was tangled, as if he didn't bother to brush it.

"Are your wings in need of repair?" he asked, leaning into the tree with his arms crossed.

I realized I didn't have a good excuse for being

here, not like this morning when I was taking Tutu for a walk.

"I was checking on the horse. Is she okay?"

He stared at me so intently I had to look away. "Beryl's fine. She's allowed to roam but doesn't usually wander that far." He spoke so quietly now I could barely hear him.

"Why were you standing behind that tree?" I asked, trying to not look away this time.

"Waiting."

I glanced around as if someone else might appear. "Waiting for what?"

He shrugged his shoulders. "For something to happen. Isn't that the point?"

"What point?"

His mouth curled a little, like he was teasing me.

"What's your name?" I asked.

"Fin," he said even more quietly, as if he were embarrassed to tell me. "And you're Chloe?"

I dropped the bike. He walked over and picked it up for me.

"How did you know my name?"

As we stood inches apart from each other, I could see he had a thick pink scar below his neck that disappeared under his shirt.

"That person who works at Birdie's told me, earlier today."

Now I was totally confused. "But Stella said you were—that you didn't—"

"Do you like honey, Chloe?"

I paused to gather my thoughts. This conversation was all over the place. I couldn't figure out if this kid was being friendly or rude or both. "Sure, I guess. Why?"

He turned to walk back into the woods. "Meet me at the farm stand tomorrow morning at ten o'clock, and there will be honey."

×××

As soon as Fin vanished, I climbed onto my bike and rode back to the store to find Stella. Why would she claim this kid couldn't talk, only to turn around and tell him my name?

I rushed through the front door, banging the bells against the wall.

"Chloe!" said Birdie. "I'm glad you came back."

"Is Stella still here?"

"Wyatt wouldn't settle down, so she had to take him up to the house." Birdie looked both ways, even though no one else was in the store. She motioned me to come closer. "Listen, I want to invite you and your family over for dinner this week. Why don't you check with your parents to see which evening works best?"

I pinched the side of my leg to keep myself from panicking. I never should have brought up an actual family. "They're traveling right now. My parents. They're camping in the mountains."

She raised her eyebrows. "You mean they left you and your sister alone?"

"She's a lot older than I am. My sister's in college. So—"

"Well, in that case, you two will have to come over for a good home-cooked meal. Tell me her name?"

"My sister's name?" I tried to come up with something new, something normal, but I couldn't help blurting out, "Viva."

"Viva? My, what an unusual name."

It was strange how saying my sister's real name felt like the lie. "She sort of made it up herself when she was learning to talk."

Another truth! What was I doing?

"That's how my name came about. My real name is

Alberta, but everyone called me Bertie for short. Only I thought they were saying *Birdie*, so I whistled whenever anyone said my name, like I was a little bird."

Something about Birdie's voice felt comforting and made me want to tell her all about Viva and the story of our names. But I knew I couldn't.

"I have to get going," I said as I turned to leave. "If you could let Stella know—"

"Now hold on a second." She picked up a notepad and pencil. "Why don't you and your sister stop over for supper this Friday? We'll all get to know each other better."

I didn't know what to say as I watched her scribble something on the notepad.

"That would be nice," I replied, "but I'll have to check with Viva."

She tore off the paper and handed it to me. "That's our address and phone number. We live a short way up the street in the lilac-blue cottage with a pair of milking cows in back. You can't miss it. Call us if you can't make it. Otherwise we'll be expecting you around six o'clock."

I folded the piece of paper several times before tucking it into my pocket. "Thank you, Mrs.—I mean, Birdie."

"It's my pleasure—especially since you've hit it off with Stella already. Lord knows," she said, glancing around again, "Stella could use a new friend."

I backed out of the door, stammering my goodbye, and took off on my bike back to the other side of the river, as if I were being chased.

Chapter 10

For the rest of the afternoon I fretted about my dilemma. Tutu and I wandered through the meadow as I thought about the best way to squirm out of dinner on Friday. I knew that even if I canceled, Birdie would probably keep inviting me, so I'd have to avoid the general store for the entire summer. And I didn't want to do that.

Something else was bothering me. Why did Stella need a new friend? More importantly, why did Birdie think the two of us could be friends? Stella had to be close to Viva's age, maybe older since she was an aunt. I didn't see how I could be friends with the sister of someone who already had a baby.

All at once, that disgusting *becoming a woman* book popped into my head along with what Mo had said about spotting. Last night, I had noticed a small stain near the seam of my shorts as I got undressed, but I quickly threw my clothes in the hamper without looking closer.

All this pacing and worrying under the hot sun was making me lightheaded. I sat down in the middle of the meadow to rest with Tutu, but she was nowhere to be seen.

"Tutu?" I called, then twisted around and yelled, *"Tutu!"*

To my relief, she stood up at the far end of the field, her stubby tail wagging slowly. She must have grown tired too and plopped down in the hay. I rushed over and scooped her up in my arms, then carried her back to the house, where we collapsed on the hammock together in the backyard.

As we rocked back and forth, I studied the bridge in the distance, trying to figure out how I was going to manage my life as Chloe. From this far away, the bridge looked so tiny it reminded me of the pieces in a board game that my family used to play. The winner was the first one who passed over a plastic moat filled with alligators.

And that's when everything became clear: *This was just a game.*

I would never see any of these people ever again

after the summer, so why worry? I should have fun with Chloe! Even Mo agreed that pretending to be a butler helped George work through his emotions, and I was essentially doing the same thing.

I could make this work. All I needed was a system to keep track of the details so that Chloe's exciting new world would stay completely separate from Agnes's pathetic old life.

Tutu was sound asleep on my stomach, so I placed her down on the patio as carefully as I could without waking her. Then I ran upstairs to get my phone and type up some notes.

It had been a couple of days since I'd checked my phone, so as soon as I powered it up, messages and voicemails from Mo appeared. I knew I should open them, but there were so many. Just thinking about my mother exhausted me. So I powered the phone down again, even more determined to ignore everything to do with my life back in Kettleboro, and shoved it in the nightstand. Then I pulled out a pen and a pad of paper and started a handwritten list:

Game: Who Am I?

Name: Chloe

Age: 14

Home: Topeka, Kansas

Occupation: actress (mostly theater, some TV ads) with
   dance background

Family: 2 MARRIED parents, 1 older sister

Mom: fashion designer

Dad: bank president

Sister: Viva, college student, not a dropout

Other: family moves and travels often

Goal: living the life I deserve.

Winner: me.

xxx

I decided to avoid going into the general store for the
rest of the week, even though I really wanted to talk
to Stella about her mysterious chat with Fin. But that
would have to wait. By staying away until Friday, I
could give Birdie the only excuse I could think of
when arriving alone for dinner.

I did manage to sneak over to the farm stand on
my bike the next morning at ten o'clock to get the

honey. I figured I would say hello to Fin, and then leave before Stella or Birdie noticed me through the big picture window. But Fin wasn't there. Instead, a paper bag with a small "C" was perched in the center of the table next to a bucket of daisies. I opened the bag and pulled out a jar of honey with the words *Fly Back Farm* printed on the label.

The sign, which listed everything for sale, didn't have a price for honey. So I wasn't sure if I was expected to put money through the cash box slot or if the honey was a gift. I had a five-dollar bill Dad had given me to buy more donuts at the general store, but I was planning on telling him they were sold out if he remembered to ask. I was really hoping he would forget anything I had ever said about this side of the bridge.

As I placed the honey back in the brown paper bag, I noticed a tiny note with even tinier handwriting taped to the bottom of the jar: *Turn right at the fork and find me at the end of the road.* It felt like a clue to something else, as if Fin was playing a game as well.

I tucked the bag inside the pouch on the back of my bike seat and took off down the dirt road. After passing the fork at the sign on the tree, I turned right, riding deeper into the woods, until the road abruptly stopped at a barbed wire fence.

A metal gate was partially open, so I laid my bike on the ground and stepped through. Beyond the dense trees, I spotted a clearing where Fin was standing in front of a row of cages. He turned as soon as he heard me walk up behind him.

"What is this place?" I asked.

A bandaged bird, huddling in the corner of one of the cages, made a squawking noise.

"A rehab facility for raptors."

We had studied raptors in science class, but I couldn't remember the various kinds other than eagles and owls. I glanced around and saw a total of four birds. Three of them were in similar metal hutches up on a platform, while one flapped around in a huge pen with netting on top.

"What's wrong with them?" I asked.

Fin removed the thick gloves he was wearing. "A lot of times, they have broken wings. Other times, it can be puncture wounds or head trauma. If it's something serious, we take them directly to the veterinarian for mending or surgery, and then they come back to us for recovery."

"What happens when they're better?"

He smiled and crossed his arms. "We release them and they fly back to wherever they belong."

As I watched Fin lock up their cages, I imagined them flying free again and I wondered how they knew where they belonged.

"So, it looks like you found the honey?"

"Oh, I almost forgot." I pulled out the five-dollar bill. "I don't know how much it costs, but—"

He swatted at a bug buzzing around his head. "No charge. You can have it. That's a jar left over from last season, but the honey's still good."

Even up close, I still couldn't figure out Fin's age. He looked about thirteen or fourteen but acted older. And his voice was so smooth and confident, like a grown-up's voice. The way he tucked his tangled hair behind his ears and slumped a little reminded me of the boys I had seen outside the high school.

He bent over to swat another bug and his shirt hung loose, so I could see more of that scar which traveled down his chest.

"Let's go down to the river," he said. "The mosquitoes aren't as bad over there."

After closing the gate, I left my bike and followed him along a path to the edge of the water where an old covered bridge crossed to the other side. Fin told me that the Hooper family had bought all the property around this bridge more than a hundred years ago, so hardly anyone knew it was down here.

It was so dark inside, like a tunnel, that I couldn't see anything. Fin pulled a penlight out of his pocket, which he said he used to examine the birds, and he pointed it at the wall. Dozens of names, initials, and dates were carved into the wooden planks.

"The oldest one is here," he said, pointing the light toward the railing. "Rob & Sadie '79."

"Really, 1979?" I asked.

"*Eighteen* seventy-nine," he said. "The bridge was built in 1878 when Rob Hooper lived here with his family. He and Sadie got married a few years later."

"Wow, that's a long time ago." I ran my fingers along the letters and numbers, trying to imagine Rob and Sadie.

We walked to the other end of the bridge and back into the sun. As we sat on the edge of the road, letting our legs dangle over the water, Fin moved closer to me. I could feel the warmth of his arm.

"Do you think people back then thought about the people who would be reading their names more than a hundred years later?" he asked.

That was an odd question. I had to think about it for a bit. "I doubt it," I replied after a second. "At least, that's not what I would be thinking about if I carved my name in that bridge."

"What would you be thinking about?"

"Probably about doing it as fast as I could, so I wouldn't get in trouble."

He nodded but didn't smile. Now I wondered what he was thinking about.

"So you aren't from around here, right?" I asked, knowing he wasn't.

He shook his head. "No, I'm from a little town outside of Montreal."

"Canada?"

"Yep. It's not far from here. About a two-hour drive north across the border. And you?"

Something made me hesitate before answering, "Kansas."

He grinned. "Are you sure?"

I could feel myself blushing. For some reason, it was harder to tell these little fibs to Fin. "My family moves around a lot."

"So you have no idea where you belong," he said. "I know how that feels."

I hadn't thought of it that way before, but he was right. I'd never felt like I belonged anywhere. Not until the day I crossed the stone bridge and became Chloe.

He picked up a pebble and tossed it in the water. Neither of us said anything for a few seconds. I assumed he must be feeling very lonely after whatever tragedy destroyed his family.

"I'm so sorry about everything," I found myself saying without thinking it through. Agnes never would have been that bold.

He pitched another pebble. "What do you mean?"

"I actually heard about your move here last winter after, you know, what happened."

He turned and looked at me. "After what happened?"

This wasn't the reaction I'd expected and realized I shouldn't have brought it up. Other than his name, I didn't know anything about Fin.

"I don't know really," I said. "It's none of my business."

"Tell me what you do know."

All I knew was what Stella had told me. Now I began to wonder if any of it was true. "That you lost your parents?"

His expression suddenly grew so serious I began to worry he might cry or get angry or throw something.

Instead, he burst out laughing. "Is that what

people think?" he asked. "That my parents died, and Harriet Hooper took me in?"

"I guess so." Now I felt embarrassed.

He took one long breath and said, "Funny thing is, I was the one who almost died, not my parents."

I glanced at the scar, just visible above his T-shirt. I wanted to ask, but figured I'd already said too much.

He threw another pebble in the river and stood up. "Almost lunchtime and I still need to clean the barn."

"Do you want some help?"

"That's okay," he said as I followed him through the wooden tunnel to the other side. "Thanks anyway."

"What about tomorrow?" I asked, surprising myself again. Chloe was so much braver than Agnes.

He stopped and stared down at me. This time I didn't look away.

"I have to go out of town for a few days," he said and smiled. "Stop by the farm stand next Monday. I'll leave something else for you, something better than honey."

I smiled back. Monday already felt like a year away.

Chapter 11

A couple of days later, Dad invited me to run errands with him after breakfast. He said he needed to stop at the college to pick up a music journal from his office, then buy some groceries. Since I'd barely had a chance to spend time with him, other than meals, I was happy to go. Especially with Fin being away for the rest of the week.

After I gave Tutu a quick walk, Dad and I took the sports car into town with the top down. Speeding up and down the rolling green hills, the wind blasting past our heads, felt almost as freeing as riding a bike.

Being on the campus in the summer months was always better than during the school year. It was less crowded, and none of my dad's adoring music students were around, just summer camp kids who didn't know him.

Dad and I hurried across the lawn, past the brick buildings covered in vines, as instruments shrieked and blasted from every window. I covered my ears and walked faster.

Dad laughed. "They're practicing," he said. "They'll get better."

I sometimes wondered if my dad was disappointed that neither Viva nor I were musical. Both of us had tried playing instruments, but nothing had ever stuck.

"Professor Moon! Timothy!"

Just when I thought we could safely cross the campus without someone hounding my dad, a bald man with a gray beard rushed toward us. He was holding a girl's hand and pulling her along. She was small but looked almost my age, which is way too old to hold an adult's hand.

"Roger!" My father beamed the way he does whenever he runs into anyone. That's why so many people like him. He makes everyone, even strangers, feel important.

"How was your sabbatical in Vienna?" asked Dad.

"Spectacular! Although Dot and I are happy to be back. Aren't we, Dot?"

I had never heard the name Dot, but it was the

perfect name for this girl. She had thin brown hair, pale skin and tiny eyes. And she wore a matching tank top and shorts set like a little kid would wear. Everything about her was skinny. Even her nose and lips were skinny. She didn't look happy at all as she clung to her father's hand.

"Agnes, this is my friend Professor Gale and his daughter Dot," said Dad. Then, as if they hadn't heard him say my name, he said, "This is my daughter Agnes. She's spending the summer with me."

Dot squinted her tiny eyes.

"I heard you were housesitting Julia's colonial on the river, you old dog!" said Roger, and the two men grinned at each other.

I forced myself to smile too, even though I didn't get their dog joke.

"Why don't you and Dot come over for supper tomorrow night?" asked Dad. "We're about to head to the grocery store. I can pick up something to grill."

Besides the fact that I couldn't imagine being stuck with this odd girl for a whole evening, tomorrow was Friday, the night I was supposed to have dinner at Stella and Birdie's house. Just as I was about to invent an excuse, Dot gave a real one.

"I'm going to my grandmother's for the weekend," she told my dad, as if he should have known that already.

Her father coughed nervously. "Then we're off to the Berkshires and Tanglewood after that, but how about the week after next?"

He looked at Dot as he said this, as if he needed her approval.

"Sounds like a plan," said Dad. "If the weather's nice, we'll eat on the patio."

As we all walked off in opposite directions, I groaned. "Are you kidding? A whole night with that weird kid?"

"Dot? She's actually quite interesting and plays the flute like a songbird. Just a bit socially awkward, that's all. Probably because she spends all her time on campus with Roger and other adults."

"Where's her mother?"

"Yvonne's an opera singer and lives in Switzerland, but she tours a lot, so Roger has full custody of Dot. Although I assume she spent some time with her mother while they were on sabbatical."

"What's a sabbatical anyway?"

Dad thought for a second. "It can be a lot of things, but generally, it's a long break from everyday life . . . a chance to get away and wipe the slate clean, and then return to your old life feeling reenergized."

"You mean, like this summer is for us?"

"I guess you're right," said Dad, as he draped his arm around my shoulders and squeezed me tight. "We're on our own sabbatical together."

The only problem was I didn't want to go back to everyday life.

×××

After Dad found the journal he needed in his office, we made it to the car without anyone else demanding his attention. We drove along a road I didn't recognize for about ten minutes, until Dad turned into a strip mall and parked in front of a drug store. It was Fred's Meds, part of the same chain where Mo worked as a pharmacist in Kettleboro.

Dad pushed the button that automatically closed the sports car roof. Then he pulled out his wallet and handed me a twenty-dollar bill.

"What's this for?"

"I thought you might need to buy some personal items at Fred's. You can meet me over at the grocery store."

I had no idea what he was talking about. "Like what? Are we out of toothpaste or something?"

His mouth curled into a crooked line like it does when he doesn't know what to say.

"Your mom called me yesterday. She's been trying to reach you on your cell phone, Agnes, but she said it always goes straight to voicemail."

I tried to act surprised, even though I had seen the long scroll of messages. "What did she want?"

"She's your mother, Agnes, and she wants to check in with you. And apparently, you forgot something on the floor of your closet. Something you might need very soon?"

The giant pink box. How did she expect me to bring it on the bus? I couldn't believe I was having this conversation with my father.

"I'm fine," I snapped. "I don't need anything."

Dad hesitated, then shifted his position so he was facing me.

"Listen, Agnes. I had a hard enough time navigating my own puberty, and I know it was far less complicated for me as a boy, at least in some ways. But if you need anything at all, you can ask me. Okay?"

Now I couldn't believe he'd said the word *puberty*, and that he was talking about himself. I dropped the twenty dollars in the cup holder and opened the car door.

"Sure. Whatever. Can we go now?"

"Wait. One more thing."

I sank into the seat, praying this had nothing to do with any other personal products from the drug store. Or that horrible book.

"Please call your mother back. You can't go the whole summer without talking to her."

"Why not? Viva hasn't talked to her, or any of us, for months."

His entire face drooped. I could tell that hurt.

"Okay, I'll call," I said and rolled my eyes. "But only if we can buy a carton of triple fudge ice cream. I've been craving chocolate lately."

Chapter 12

The next day, I left for Stella and Birdie's house a few minutes before six, making a quick stop at the farm stand. The vegetable crates were empty and covered up with square boards. Even the cash box and the *Fly Back Farm* sign were gone. It almost felt as if Fin wasn't coming back, but something inside me knew that wasn't the case, that I could trust him.

Dad and I usually ate dinner around seven. Some nights I was back early and helped him cook, but most nights I pulled into the driveway on my bike just in time to eat. I figured if I ate dinner really fast with Stella and Birdie at six o'clock, I could still arrive home a little late for our supper at seven o'clock and he'd never know. And I had the perfect excuse to leave Stella and Birdie's house early. The same excuse for being away from the store all week.

"Chloe!" Stella called out.

She was standing in front of their lilac-blue house with Wyatt on her hip, watching me ride up the road. A couple of cows were behind an old wooden fence munching on grass, and a tall church steeple poked above the trees beyond their backyard.

"We weren't sure if you were going to make it, since we hadn't seen you all week. But I'm really glad you did."

I pushed my bike up the gravel driveway and leaned it against the fence.

"Where's your sister? Is she coming later?" asked Stella, who couldn't seem to stop talking.

"She's sick," I finally said. I had practiced the story in my head a dozen times, so I knew exactly what to say. "That's why I haven't stopped by the store."

"Shoot. I'm sorry to hear that." She pulled her phone out of her pocket and Wyatt immediately lunged for it. "I should have your number."

I didn't want to let her get that close to Agnes, plus I didn't want to admit I had an old phone that I hardly ever checked. "Mine's broken."

"Really? Man, you're having a tough week, Chloe." She patted me on the back, which made me feel a little guilty, but also relieved that my excuses had worked.

Wyatt began to squirm, so Stella set him down on the ground. He toddled ahead of us through the front door and down the hall to the kitchen. Chicken was frying in a pan of oil and the smell made me hungry. Birdie wore an old-fashioned apron, the kind with frills along the edges, and the table was already set. Her glasses had steamed up from all the cooking, so she took them off and wiped them with the corner of her apron.

"Her sister's sick," Stella announced as she took a carrot from a bowl of raw vegetables and handed one to Wyatt. "Go on and watch your Froggy show. The grown-ups want to talk."

It felt strange being included with the grown-ups.

Birdie dropped a handful of napkins on the table. "Oh no. And with your parents away in the mountains. What's she got?"

"Well, that's the thing," I said, "we aren't sure."

I thought it would be better to go with a mysterious sickness rather than something specific, in case I got tripped up on the details.

Stella flopped into a chair and pulled out the seat next to hers for me to sit.

"Has she been to a doctor?" asked Birdie.

"Lots of doctors," I replied. "It's been going on

for a long time. Some weeks she's fine, other weeks she feels terrible. No one really knows what's wrong with her."

Birdie looked concerned. "What are her symptoms when she feels terrible?"

My heart skipped a beat. I hadn't expected so many questions. "Headaches, and uh, sometimes stomachaches. Her back hurts and she gets dizzy a lot."

"Goodness, that sounds awful," said Birdie. "She should see a specialist if it's been going on a long time."

I didn't mean for it to sound awful, just convincing.

Luckily, the front door opened and a man with thick, wavy hair entered the kitchen. He had a big smile on his face, but his clothes were filthy. Wyatt squealed with delight and clung to the bottom of his leg.

"This is that new girl I was telling you about," said Stella. "Chloe, this is my brother, Dave."

"Hey there, Chloe. Nice to meet you."

I was so surprised this adult stranger knew about me I could barely look him in the eye. But then I remembered that Chloe was much more confident and outgoing than Agnes.

"It's nice to meet you too."

Dave bent down and picked up Wyatt by his ankles, then twisted him through a series of fun flips and turns.

"How long till we eat?" asked Dave, swinging Wyatt onto his shoulders. "I need to clean up before dinner."

"Everything's almost ready," said Birdie. "But we can wait a few extra minutes if you want to take a quick shower."

After Dave and Wyatt disappeared up the stairs, Birdie poured two glasses of lemonade.

"Take these out on the front porch, girls, and get to know each other better."

At that moment, I relaxed. Everything about this family made me feel at home, plus I liked being treated like an adult. It was nice to sit on the porch with Stella and chat about stuff like grown-ups do.

I found out Dave was Wyatt's dad, which wasn't hard to guess, even though they didn't look anything alike. Stella said Dave was a mechanic and owned an auto repair shop, which was why his clothes were so dirty.

"Birdie and I take care of Wyatt during the day while Dave's at work," Stella explained. "Next year, when Wyatt turns three, he can go to the local preschool."

I couldn't help asking, "Does Wyatt's mom work too?"

Stella frowned. "She doesn't have much to do with him other than drop off presents on his birthday and holidays. She was there at the conception and birth, of course, but she didn't want the responsibility."

All at once, I *didn't* want to chat about grown-up stuff. Anything to do with babies and pregnancies reminded me of Mo and her gross lectures and that stupid pink box.

The screen door swung open—perfect timing again. "The boys are ready, so come on in and wash your hands, ladies," said Birdie, "and let's eat."

Stella scooped potato salad onto her plate, then passed the bowl to me, as she told us about Wyatt's latest fascination with a new game on her phone that made farm animal noises. Wyatt was banging the tray of his high chair with a little spoon, but as soon as he heard his name mentioned he stopped—and began to moo. This made everyone laugh, except Birdie. As she helped herself to green beans, she insisted that Wyatt was never going to learn to talk if he kept poking at the cell phone all day.

Sitting together at the dinner table, chatting and laughing and passing food to each other, reminded me of how it used to feel to be a family. Back then, I never would have realized how much I would miss this.

After we finished dinner and the dishes were cleared, I glanced up at the kitchen clock and saw that it was five minutes past seven. I popped up and slid my chair against the table a little too fast.

"Everything was delicious, but I have to get going. I told Viva I'd be back by now."

They all looked surprised.

"You gobbled up that potato salad," said Birdie, grinning. "Would you like to take some home?"

I shook my head. "It was great, but we have lots of food in the fridge."

"What about dessert?" said Stella. "You gotta stay for pie."

"And ice cream, I hope," added Dave. He looked gigantic sitting next to his tiny son.

Birdie stood and went over to the cupboard where she took out a paper plate, some tin foil, and a bag.

"Chloe's right. She needs to get home to that sick sister of hers. At least let me wrap up some pie for you to take back."

Stella walked with me out to my bike. I decided

this was a good chance to bring up something that had been bugging me.

"By the way, I met Fin," I said.

"Who?" She sat on the bottom step of their porch as I tied the bag filled with pie around my handlebars, which I'd have to ditch before dinner with my dad.

"That boy who you said couldn't talk? His voice is quiet, but he can definitely talk. And his parents are alive and well."

"They are?" Her big eyes doubled in size. "Well, that's a relief."

"And he said you told him my name?"

She shook her head. "That's impossible. I've never heard that kid say a word, much less ask me anything."

"Well then, how did he know my name?"

"Beats me." She shrugged. "Maybe he's psychic."

I didn't know who to believe. Both Stella and Fin seemed so convincing.

Just then we heard Wyatt cry loudly, like he'd fallen down and hurt himself.

Stella jumped up. "I gotta go, Chloe," she said and rushed through the door as if no one else was inside to help him. "See ya later!"

Chapter 13

Monday morning couldn't come soon enough. After I fed Tutu and ate my breakfast, I hopped on my bike and rode toward the bridge as fast as I could. I was excited to see what was waiting for me at the farm stand, but I really wanted to know why Fin might have lied to me—even though I had lied to him about a lot more things.

The *Fly Back Farm* sign was back on top of the stand, which was a relief, and the crates were overflowing with vegetables. Just as before, a paper bag with the letter C was sitting on the table, this time next to the strawberries. The bag felt heavy, so I was anxious to see what it could be. I opened it and peered in.

"Yuck."

A bunch of crooked, muddy carrots with dirty green leaves was stuffed inside. I couldn't figure out how this could be better than honey . . . until I saw a note, again written in tiny letters, buried at the bottom.

Meet me at the farm by the barn, and bring Beryl's favorite snack.

Across the street, the door to the general store flew open. Birdie stepped out into the sun holding her hand over her eyes. "Morning, Chloe! How's your sister doing?"

I clutched the paper bag against my side as she strolled toward me. "She's much better today. Thank you for dinner on Friday."

Birdie smiled. "We'll have to do it again when your parents get back."

I didn't know what to say, so I said nothing and looked down at the bag.

"Picking up some of those divine strawberries?" she asked.

I nodded, which felt less like a lie than it would answering out loud.

"You're awfully quiet—everything all right?"

"I'm fine, just thinking about a few things I have to get done."

She reached into a pocket hidden along the seam of her dress and placed a delicate silver chain on the counter by the lettuce.

"Well, I won't keep you then. I heard this is your bracelet. I keep forgetting to give it to you."

I stared at it—tiny glass beads woven through a thin chain. "It's pretty, but it's not mine."

"How peculiar," said Birdie. "That boy living with Harriet Hooper brought it to the store a week or so ago, thinking it was yours. He didn't know your name, so he asked if I could give it to you."

It hadn't occurred to me that Birdie, not Stella, had told Fin my name. So both of them had been telling the truth. But why would Fin think the bracelet was mine before we'd even met?

"You know, Harriet should put a Lost and Found basket on this farm stand," she said. "Heaven knows, a lot of people around here could use one of those."

It sounded like she was talking about more than a misplaced bracelet.

Across the street a customer entered the store.

Birdie sighed. "I'd better get going."

"Thanks again for dinner," I said as she turned to leave. "It was nice to meet Wyatt's father."

She stopped and looked back. "When did you meet Wyatt's father?"

Now I was confused. "At your house. Your grandson, Dave? Wyatt's dad?"

"Oh, Dave," she said softly. "That's right, you met Dave. My mind gets so jumbled lately."

Birdie held onto the edges of her dress with both hands as she continued back across the street.

"No one's at the cash register," she called over her shoulder as she waved. "Toodaloo!"

I pedaled slowly down the dirt road, pinching the bag of dirty carrots between my fingers. I realized I had no idea why Stella lived with her grandmother. In fact, she hadn't mentioned her parents once. I wondered if something tragic had happened to them, and that was why she'd assumed the same of Fin. It would explain why Birdie felt Stella needed a new friend.

After turning left at the fork, in the direction of the farm, I kept a close eye on the dense trees along the road. Fin was so unpredictable, I half expected him to jump out of the woods at any moment. But he didn't.

Two stone posts marked the entrance to the farm. A rusty chain hung close to the ground between the posts. I leaned my bike against a knotted tree and stepped over the chain.

The thick bushes suddenly opened into a clearing. In the distance, up a steep slope, stood a small white farmhouse, and to the left of that was a gray barn, where I was supposed to meet Fin. But how would he know that I was here?

Flowers grew everywhere, rows and rows of them. I had never seen so many in one place. I watched as butterflies sifted through the blossoms.

"May I help you?"

A pretty woman with curly, sand-colored hair stood up between two of the garden rows. I wondered if I was in the wrong place.

"Does Fin live here?"

She brushed off her hands and walked toward me. "I'm Harriet Hooper," she said. "How do you know Fin?"

This woman was not how I'd pictured Harriet Hooper. For one thing, she didn't look that much older than Viva.

"We met a couple weeks ago when I was walking my dog. She's not my dog really, but I'm taking care of her for the summer. Tutu."

"Tutu?"

"That's the dog's name."

Then I bit my lip as I caught my mistake. I shouldn't have said anything about Tutu if I wanted to keep Agnes far away on the other side.

Harriet laughed. "So what's your name?"

I clutched the bag of carrots with both hands. "Chloe."

"Such a beautiful name."

I tried to smile, but now I felt a little nervous.

"What've you got there, Chloe?"

This Harriet person asked a lot of questions.

"Um. It's something that—"

"*Harriet!*" Fin called from the front porch up the hill. "Phone for you."

He leaned against the railing, his hands cupped around his mouth. The morning sun made his red hair glow, like it was on fire.

"Well, there he is! Excuse me, Chloe. It was nice meeting you."

She hurried toward the house, passing Fin on his way down. They paused for a second and said something to each other that I couldn't hear. He jogged the rest of the way and stopped a few feet in front of me.

"How was your trip?" I asked.

"Fine. I see you found the carrots."

I thrust the bag toward him, forcing him to move closer and take it. "They're dirty," I said with a grin.

"Because they just came out of the ground." He

brushed my hand as he took the bag. "That's the way horses like them, fresh."

Up on the porch, the screen door slammed.

"Who was on the phone?" Harriet called down to Fin. "They hung up."

The corners of his mouth curled. "Must have been a sales call."

I wondered if the phone had rung at all.

"Hey Chloe," Harriet said more loudly, "do you want to stay for lunch?"

"Sure, thanks," I called back before Fin could say anything. He rolled his eyes.

"What's the matter?" I asked. "You don't want me to stay for lunch?"

He stared at me in that way of his, like he could read my mind, making it hard to look him in the eye. "You can stay if you want."

I followed him down a path toward the barn. We passed four large wooden boxes with drawers covered in bees, and I jumped to the side.

"They won't bother you. They're busy making honey. You can practically touch the hives and they won't do anything."

As soon as Fin slid the barn door open, Beryl stepped out into the light and trotted toward a patch of tall grass to graze. In the distance, chickens were pecking at the ground near a couple of geese.

"Nothing is tied up around here? Every animal is loose."

"This is their home," said Fin. "It's where they want to be. But if they decide to leave, they can use their wings and fly away."

"Except for the horse."

He glanced toward the field. "She used to fly. She won races all over the world. That's how she got her name."

"Beryl?"

"Named after Beryl Markham, the first woman to fly solo from Europe across the Atlantic. She also trained racehorses."

"What happened to her?"

"Which one?"

"Both, I guess."

"The original Beryl broke her leg in old age and died. This Beryl injured her leg too, during a race. But she was saved from a dire ending by Harriet, who helped her heal. Harriet claims Beryl has done the same for her."

He opened the paper bag and whistled toward the horse. Her ears perked up as she ambled over.

Fin handed me a carrot. "Hold your hand flat like this."

Her thick lips felt like dough. I didn't feel her teeth at all as she took the whole carrot with one bite. Then she pressed her soft nose under my arm searching for more. I took another carrot from the bag and held out my hand again.

"Do you want to go for a ride?" Fin asked.

"Right now? But she doesn't have a saddle."

I had never been on a horse, but I couldn't decide if I should admit that to Fin. Maybe Chloe would know exactly what to do.

"You can ride her bareback. Since she can't run anymore, she's totally mellow."

He bent down a little, wove his fingers together, and cupped his hands. Agnes never would have stepped onto his palms, but Chloe did.

"Hold onto her mane."

At first I felt unsteady sitting on such a large animal. Her back was smooth and wide, but her bony spine felt delicate running between my legs. Beryl followed Fin as he wandered slowly around the property. The ride was bumpier than I thought it would be, and I wished I'd worn jeans because my legs were starting to itch. But after a few minutes I relaxed into her warm body. Then I leaned forward and wrapped my arms around her strong neck.

The screen door slammed again, startling me awake as if I'd been dreaming.

"Sandwiches are ready!" Harriet called from the porch.

I let Fin answer this time.

"Be right there," he replied, then held out his hands to help me down.

×××

Every corner of their house held something wonderful, like a clay vase full of daisies and a beautiful glass sculpture and a basket filled with peaches.

The smell of toast floated from the kitchen as Harriet appeared holding two plates.

"Hope you like basil, Chloe. I planted way too much of it this year."

Fin whispered, "We eat basil at every meal."

"I heard that," said Harriet.

The large room was filled with windows overlooking the gardens and the barn. I could see that Beryl and the chickens had roamed part way up the hill as they nibbled at the ground.

Both Fin and Harriet took a bite of their sandwiches at the same time. Before I took a bite of mine, I had to ask, "So are you two cousins or something like that?"

Harriet chewed slowly as she glanced sideways at Fin.

He wiped his mouth with his napkin before answering. "Something like that."

Harriet coughed and cleared her throat. "I forgot drinks. What would you like, Chloe? Milk? Juice?"

"Water would be great, thanks."

As soon as she walked away, I said, "I guess I shouldn't have asked that."

"It's fine," said Fin. "It's just complicated."

I could tell I needed to drop the subject.

"So I heard you thought I lost a bracelet?"

He glanced at my empty wrist, then shifted in his chair. "I have a confession to make, Chloe. That day you were staring at me through the store window, I really wanted to meet you. So when I found the bracelet by the side of the road, I pretended it was yours."

I didn't know what to say. No one had ever wanted to get to know me, not like that.

"Sorry," he added. "It wasn't exactly an honest way of starting out."

Fortunately, Harriet returned with two glasses before I had to respond. But her face was blotchy as if she had been crying. She dabbed her nose with a tissue and tried to smile.

"So tell me, do you live near here, Chloe?"

"No," I said. "My family is visiting for the summer."

"She's from Kansas," said Fin.

Hearing him repeat my fibs made me even more uncomfortable.

"Like Dorothy!" Harriet suddenly brightened. "Do you live on the other side of the rainbow?"

She laughed at her own joke and Fin groaned.

Something about their relationship seemed familiar but tense. Like my relationship with Viva. I studied their similar faces and wondered if Harriet could be Fin's much older sister, or maybe a half-sister.

"So why does everything on your farm have wings?" I asked, hoping to steer the conversation away from me.

She took another bite of her sandwich before answering. "Mainly as a reminder," said Harriet, "that we all have the power to fly."

"We do?"

She nodded. "Different beings have different ways of flying, but it's inside all of us."

I thought about that for a second. "Fly where?"

"That depends on you," said Harriet. "Sometimes, we need to fly away from where we came from, from what we've known, from where we've been stuck. And sometimes, we need to fly back home."

Fin stood up, holding his empty dish. "Chloe didn't stay for lunch in order to hear your philosophy on life." The tone of his voice startled both of us. He looked down at me and asked, "Are you done eating?"

It seemed clear that I had stumbled into a family issue. I recognized all the signs from my own family. That way of saying things without saying them directly.

We handed our dishes to Fin. He shuffled down the hall toward the kitchen, carrying the three plates stacked on top of each other.

Harriet put her hand on mine and lowered her voice.

"I know he seems upset, but he's working through a lot of emotions. I'm so glad he's found someone like you to talk to, Chloe. Fin has been through so much over the past year. More than anyone his age should have to deal with. Anyway, I can tell you're already a good friend to him."

Exactly what Birdie had said about Stella.

What was going on around here? And why did everyone think I was such a good friend? I wasn't even the person they thought I was.

Chapter 14

I started hanging out with Fin almost every day. On the one hand, I felt like I already knew a lot about him, but at the same time, he seemed to have so many secrets. I didn't want to ask him too many questions, though, in case he would start asking *me* too many questions. I wasn't ready to put an end to my little game and confess the truth about myself.

A few days after lunch with Harriet, Fin and I wandered down the dirt road to check on the raptors. A small falcon and a hawk were the only birds in rehab at the moment and both were doing well, soon to be freed.

"So how does it work?" I asked. "Do you fling open their cages and tell them to sign out at the front desk?"

He smirked. "Very funny. We actually release them as close as possible to wherever they were rescued. But we don't know where these two were found, so we'll bring them up the mountain behind the farm. The hawk prefers the woods, so he'll be released in the trees, but we'll bring the little falcon to the top where it's nice and open."

"And they take off like nothing ever happened?"

"No, they usually hang out for a couple hours to get their bearings. But once they're ready to go, it's incredible to watch them take flight again, all on their own. When they're released at the top of the mountain, sometimes you can watch them soar for a long time—over the treetops, across the river, and down through the valley—until they disappear from sight."

The way Fin described it, staring off into the distance, made it sound amazing.

"Can I come and help?"

"I don't know," he said, as he locked up their cages. "Legally you have to be eighteen years old to get a wildlife permit."

A jolt of shock ran through my body. "Are *you* eighteen years old?"

He laughed. "I'm only fifteen, so technically I'm

not allowed to handle the birds on my own either. I can't wait to get licensed in three years."

I tried to listen to him, but I didn't hear anything after he said he was fifteen. I'd assumed he was a year or so older than I was, but I never would have guessed he was three years older.

"So, you're in high school?" I asked.

He took off the heavy leather gloves and tucked them in a metal box. "I've always been home schooled for various reasons," he said and crossed his arms in that way he did when he was getting serious. "Why? Are you older than fifteen?"

I gulped. "Nope."

"Because I assumed you were like fourteen? No offense, you're really smart and interesting, but you have a sweet way about you that makes you seem a little younger."

I could feel myself blush.

"Don't be embarrassed," he said. "I don't care if you're only fourteen. Really, Chloe. You're a lot more mature than most girls I know. It's just a number."

I realized he was right, but at the same time, his age made me think differently about him. About us.

One rainy afternoon, Dad suggested we go to the movies. He said he was tired of writing and needed a break. We drove to a mall near the grocery store to watch a superhero film. The theater was already dark by the time we sat down. Dad held a bucket of greasy popcorn between us. The first previews blasted onto the screen and right away, a little kid began to cry.

"Why do people bring babies to the movies?" Dad whispered.

I laughed. "Maybe because we're watching a kids' film?"

Near the front of the theater, a woman with a shrieking little boy in her arms stood and slid past the others in her row. As she hurried up the aisle, I was shocked to see it was Stella carrying Wyatt. I slipped down into my seat and turned away.

"Agnes?" said Dad. "Are you feeling all right?"

I paused for a second, waiting for them to pass. "I'm not sure."

He leaned against my shoulder. "Do you need to leave, honey?"

"Maybe."

He waited for me to make a decision, but I didn't know what to do. It had never occurred to me that my two worlds could actually collide.

"Headache or stomachache?" Dad whispered.

I said the only thing I knew would sound convincing. "Cramps."

Two minutes later Stella returned, rushing down the dark aisle with Wyatt, who was quietly holding a large box of candy. The theater wasn't even half full so there was a good chance she'd see me when the lights went on at the end.

"It's your call," said Dad. "I'm fine either way."

I felt terrible ruining his one day off. He'd been working so hard lately that he'd barely had a chance to ride his bike. But I knew I couldn't risk Stella spotting me. "I think we'd better go."

The rain was pouring, so we were soaked by the time we climbed inside the little green car. On the drive back to the house, neither of us said a word. The windshield wipers didn't work very well, so Dad had to squint, concentrating extra hard on the road. By the time we pulled in our driveway, the downpour had slowed to a drizzle. I turned to open my door, but Dad took my hand.

"Agnes. Why haven't you called your mother yet?"

Apparently, Mo was still leaving Dad messages about my lack of communication and was starting to blame him.

I didn't know how to explain to Dad that I didn't want anything to do with my old life. So I said nothing and stared at my lap.

"If you're getting cramps this bad, you should let her know," he added. "I'm really not an expert in that field. Mo is the one who can answer any questions you might have."

"Okay, okay," I groaned. "I'll call her."

"Now?" he asked. "Please?"

I felt so guilty about ruining our one afternoon together, I agreed. So as soon as I was back in my bedroom, I braced myself and powered up my phone.

"For Godzilla's sake, *Agnes Moon*! I've been worried sick about you. Why haven't you called or sent me one single text?!"

Hearing my mother say my name made my entire body cramp. "I've been really busy, Mo. So, how's Kansas?"

"Kansas is fine, thank you very much. In fact, Kansas is fabulous if you want to know the truth. And little Georgie is having the time of his life, which could have been the same for you if you'd given Topeka a chance. Everyone loves Richard's murals. He's the talk of the town!"

"That's nice."

"So what could possibly be keeping you so busy that you can't find a moment to send your only mother a quick photo or a text to let her know you're alive?"

"Of course I'm alive. I'm pretty sure Dad would let you know if I'd died."

"Always the wise cracker!"

I wanted more than anything to get off the phone, but then Mo insisted I say hello to George.

"Top of the day to you!" he blurted way too loudly in his stupid butler voice.

"Hello, George. Now put Mo back on the phone."

"Isn't he a pistol?" said Mo. "That kid is going to take the world by storm just like his father."

Somehow my mother always managed to say exactly the wrong thing at exactly the wrong moment.

"I have to go, Mo."

"Wait. What about Timothy? Is he feeling okay? He sounds okay."

"Of course he's okay."

"So the illness . . . ?"

Ugh. I had completely forgotten about the whole reason for this summer happening at all.

"He's, uh, pretty much recovered, I think," I replied. "He doesn't like to talk about it."

"Figures!" she said dryly. "That apple doesn't fall far from the tree."

"Don't worry about us, Mo. He's fine and I'm fine."

"You don't sound fine."

"I'm more than fine! I have a little headache, that's all."

"Another sign of oncoming menstruation. I hope your father bought you a new box of pads?"

"Oh no, you're breaking up. I can't hear you. I'd better go, Mo. Bye!"

What started off as a great day had now become just another crummy episode in Agnes's doomed life. There was no way I was going back to that.

Chapter 15

Fin went away again, but this time he promised that when he got back, he would tell me where he kept going. He had been very secretive about these trips. I worried they might have something to do with that scar down his chest.

Lately I had been avoiding the general store, because Stella always asked about my sister. I could tell she needed a friend closer to her age, and I wondered why she didn't seem to have any. Then one morning, while Fin was gone, Dad discovered we were out of bread and asked if I could ride my bike across the bridge to the general store and pick up a loaf before lunch. As I parked my bike and twisted my hair into a bun, Stella poked her head outside and held the front door open for me.

"Chloe, I'm so glad you're here. Could you do me

a huge favor?" she asked as I entered the store. "I need an extra pair of hands for an hour or two. We're catering a Rotary Club meeting tonight and Wyatt's got a cold, so Birdie has to stay home with him."

I wondered why Dave didn't stay home with Wyatt, since he was his father. "I didn't know you made anything other than donuts."

"We do preorders for small and medium-size events. Nothing fancy. The store makes hardly any money these days, so we have to bring in business any way we can. I could really use some help if you have time."

"Sure, I can help. I'm pretty good at cooking."

"You're the best!" She handed me an apron and added, "It must be so nice being rich."

It took me a few seconds to realize she was talking about me. Chloe. "Not really. My parents are gone a lot."

She didn't say anything, which reminded me how she never mentioned anything about her parents.

"So do your folks live with you?" I asked. "I didn't get to meet them at your house."

She bent behind the counter and pulled out a sign to place by the cash register instructing people to ring the bell for service.

"My mother took off a long time ago and my father remarried someone who wanted nothing to do with me or Dave. So we moved in with Birdie."

"Wow. I'm sorry," I said. "I didn't know that."

The more I got to know Stella, the more she seemed to have in common with Agnes. If only I could tell her that.

"It's okay." She sighed, like it was all a big inconvenience, but I knew how much it had to hurt.

The back kitchen had long wooden counters and high cabinets that reached almost to the ceiling. Stella handed me a large stainless steel bowl and took a recipe card out of her apron pocket.

"Remember how much you liked Birdie's potato salad? It's pretty easy to make and I already cooked the potatoes. You'll find the other ingredients in the refrigerator. I'm going to mix up a batch of her world-famous cheddar bites."

"What are those?"

"They're like mini biscuits, loaded with cheese and butter. Everybody loves them."

After the potato salad was done, Stella handed me Birdie's special recipe for brownies and asked me to mix up enough batter for four pans. The secret ingredient was marshmallow fluff, which apparently made them extra gooey.

We hardly spoke all morning, since Stella was working on the more complicated dishes and running around getting everything else organized, like paper plates and tablecloths. Just as I slid the last pan of brownies into the oven, someone rang the bell. Stella rushed out front to help the customer while I washed the stack of bowls and utensils.

As I reached for a dish towel, I heard a familiar voice. I moved closer toward the swinging door to listen.

"Her name is Agnes. She's twelve and has long, thick hair. She was supposed to pick up bread?"

My dad! I had forgotten all about the bread.

"I don't know anyone like that," I heard Stella say. "She didn't come in here."

"That's strange," said Dad. "I thought she meant this store, but maybe it's a different one."

"McGrath's is on Palmer Lane, about a half mile up that way. They sell mostly hardware stuff, but they have groceries too."

"Thanks," said Dad. "I'll drive up there to check."

The front door closed and in a flash of panic,

I remembered my bike. Luckily I had tucked it along the side of the building, so Dad probably wouldn't see it as he left.

Stella almost hit me with the swinging door as she charged back into the kitchen. "Just some guy looking for his kid," she said. Then added, "Man, those brownies smell good, Chloe! I don't know what I would've done without your help. You know, while you're here, there's something I really need to tell you."

She started to blink so much she had to remove her glasses and wipe her eyes. I had no idea what Stella needed to tell me, but it didn't matter. I knew I had to get back to the house before Dad did.

"Can we meet up later? I didn't realize it was so late and I have to go and"—I hesitated to make sure I didn't give away anything—"feed my rabbit. I didn't get a chance to before I left this morning."

"Oh, sure. I didn't even know you had a pet rabbit," she said as she slid her glasses back into place. "Anyway, thanks again for being such a life saver, Chloe. I really can't wait to meet that sister of yours someday, especially if she's as sweet as you."

xxx

All I could think about was Dad driving around searching for me. And how he'd almost found me on this side of the bridge. I must have broken some record as I raced home and dropped my bike against the big maple tree in front of the porch. On my way in I grabbed Tutu and curled up with her on the couch. A small book was on the coffee table, and I opened it to the middle pages so it would look like I'd been reading for a while.

Less than five minutes later the green sports car roared into the driveway.

"Agnes!" said Dad, bounding in from the porch. He shoved open the screen door so hard it banged into the wall. "Where have you been?"

"Huh?" I mumbled, pretending to read the book. "Out riding my bike."

He took a deep breath. I could tell he didn't want to come off as the worried parent. "That sounds nice, but you were supposed to be home two hours ago with a loaf of bread?"

"Oops. Forgot. Sorry about that."

He stood frozen a few seconds more, then opened the cabinet and took out a bowl. "That's okay. I'll have cereal for lunch. Do you want some?"

"I'm good, thanks."

Dad always took his lunch up to his office to keep working, but this time he lingered, leaning against the counter. "It would be great if you could keep your phone on you when you're out on your rides, in case I need to get ahold of you."

Even though he believed kids should be free to explore on their own, he was probably wondering if he'd given me too much freedom. "Sure. I'll try to remember."

"Great. Thanks." After another few seconds he said, "So where'd you go on your bike?"

"I don't know. Around."

A puff of wind blew all the curtains up into the air at the same time.

"So that store you visit over in Renew? Is it Birdie's or McGrath's?"

I knew I couldn't admit it was Birdie's. I rolled on my side. "Dad! I'm trying to read."

"Oh, of course."

He placed the bowl in the sink and headed toward the stairs.

"I almost forgot," he added. "Roger and Dot are coming over for dinner tomorrow night. Make sure you're home by six, okay? No losing track of time."

I groaned at the mention of Dot, but secretly I was very relieved to put an end to his questions. "I guess."

"*I guess* isn't an answer."

Tutu licked my face, as if she wanted us to stop arguing.

"Okay, whatever. I'll be on time, Dad."

He climbed halfway up the stairs, then turned around again. "Since when have you become a fan of Robert Frost?"

"Who?"

"The book." He pointed at the cover. "Are you enjoying his poems?"

"Oh yeah. They're pretty good," I said. "But you're making it hard to concentrate."

Chapter 16

They arrived exactly at six. On the dot.

Roger handed Dad a plate covered in foil. "A little something for dessert. Dot is a whiz at making chocolate chip cookies!"

We all looked at Dot, who was wearing another matching short and shirt set.

"It's from a package," she replied. "Anyone could make them as long as they have two eggs, a stick of butter, and water." She glanced over at Tutu, who was sleeping in the corner, and added, "I'm allergic to dogs."

Roger chuckled nervously and said, "Only if you touch them, honey. You'll be fine if you keep your distance."

"Easy for you to say," said Dot. "I'm going out to the car to get my nose spray."

We ate grilled burgers, coleslaw, and watermelon at the round glass table on the patio. The two dads talked nonstop about classical concerts and instruments and teaching. Once in a while they would try to include Dot and me in the conversation, but I had no interest in music and Dot didn't seem interested in anything.

"Did I tell you I saw that cello prodigy, von Zimmermann, perform in Vienna last fall at the International Youth competition, days before his breakdown?" said Roger. "Too bad your favorite conductor wasn't able to recruit him."

Dad cleared his throat and coughed a few times.

"Who's your favorite conductor?" I asked, curious to hear more.

"You mean they haven't met?" said Roger.

Dad stood up and clapped his hands together. "Hey! Time for those cookies. What do you say, Dot?"

"I'm full," announced Dot. Then, for the first time all evening, she looked directly at me and spoke. "Can I see your bedroom, Agnes?"

×××

I opened the door and let her enter first. As she moved slowly around the room, she bobbed her head up and down, like it was her job to approve of everything.

"Thanks for getting me out of there," I said, even though I didn't want to be with her here. "Music is so boring, especially the cello. It's all my dad talks about."

Suddenly, she dropped onto my bed, landing flat on her back, her arms and legs spread across the covers.

"Are you okay, Dot?"

After a few more seconds of silence she announced, "I hate my mother."

For some reason, this statement didn't surprise me at all coming from Dot. I sat on the cushy pink chair near one of the tall windows.

"I kind of hate my mother too," I said. But as soon as I said it, I realized it wasn't true.

Dot shot up and crisscrossed her legs. "You do?"

"Not really. She's just unbelievably annoying."

She thought about it, then asked, "Does she love you?"

That question did surprise me. I shrugged my shoulders. "Of course. I mean, don't all mothers have to love their kids?"

Dot slumped and began picking at the bedspread. "Not mine. She wishes I was never born."

This conversation had gotten very awkward very fast. I didn't even know this girl. And I definitely didn't want to get to know her. "I'm sure that's not true. Do you want to go and get some dessert?"

"It's true," she blurted. "I heard her say it when my father and I visited her in Switzerland. They thought I was outside in the garden when they were arguing, but I was in the bathroom and heard every word. My father said it was my mother's turn to take me for a couple years and she refused. She said her singing career took up every second of her life and she hadn't wanted me in the first place and that it was his fault I was even born."

Dot curled up on her side and buried her head under my pillow.

I couldn't imagine hearing something like that. I felt a little sorry for Dot, even though I still didn't like her.

"I'm playing a secret game," I confessed, to get her mind off her parents.

She emerged from the covers and sat up. "What kind of secret game?"

It actually felt good to finally tell someone. And it wasn't like Dot knew anyone that I knew, other than my dad. "You have to swear you won't tell anyone."

"I swear," she answered quickly.

I lowered my voice and leaned toward her.

"There are people who think I'm a completely different person. With a different life in another state. I even have a different name."

She scrunched her face. "They don't know your name is Agnes?"

"Nope. They think I'm Chloe."

For the first time since I'd met Dot, she smiled. "Can I call you Chloe?"

I thought about it for a second.

"I guess so, but not in front of our dads."

She dropped her legs over the side of the bed and kicked the air. "And you can call me Vladlena."

"What? Why would you want anyone to call you that?"

"Vladlena Smirnov was a little-known flutist born in the former Soviet Union during the Cold War, who could have been the most famous flutist in the world had her circumstances been different."

I tried not to roll my eyes. This kid was certifiably strange. I wondered if I had made a mistake confiding in Dot. It was too late now. Hopefully, I'd never see her again after tonight.

"Okay, Vladlena," I whispered. "Now let's go downstairs and eat some of those chocolate chip cookies."

As we left the bedroom, she held my hand like a little kid. I tried pulling away, but she wouldn't let go.

xxx

The next morning I twisted my hair back and rode my bike over to the farm stand to see if Fin had left anything for me yet. He promised he'd leave me an even better surprise to let me know that he was back. I searched everywhere, even under the empty crates, but found nothing. A week had passed and hardly anything was for sale, other than some spotted yellow squash and overripe tomatoes. I was starting to worry something was wrong.

On top of that, I was having a hard time getting Dot out of my head. Dad told me at breakfast that he'd already received an email from Roger saying he'd never seen Dot happier. And that he wanted to know when the four of us could get together again.

I explained to Dad that I was just being nice to her so she would stop acting weird and moody, and that I had no interest in seeing her again. Actually, I was still upset about what she'd told me about her mother, and I didn't want to think about it anymore.

"Hey Chloe!"

I turned around. Stella was standing in front of the store holding the door open.

"You want to go swimming this afternoon?" she called. "There's a beach down the river not far from here."

I picked up my bike and pushed it across the road. "I don't have a suit."

Like a bad dream, that dreadful mother-daughter shopping day with Mo flashed through my mind. Even though it seemed so long ago.

"Well, you can wear shorts," said Stella, which was the best thing about her. She always made everything feel so easy. "There's an ice cream truck too!" she added. "My treat. I owe you for helping yesterday. And now we can talk some more."

I remembered Stella had wanted to share something with me when we were cooking, but I wasn't sure I wanted to hear it. Having an older friend like Stella made me feel older, but also uneasy. As if I would be expected to understand things I knew nothing about.

But since Fin was still away, and I was trying to get Dot out of my head, I agreed to meet her at the middle of the bridge after lunch.

Stella wore shorts too, instead of a bathing suit,

and we both draped our towels around our necks. To my surprise, we walked along the river on the Bittersweet side of the bridge, across the water from Renew. It felt dangerous being Chloe on this side, like I might mess up or get caught.

"Isn't there a beach over in Renew?" I asked.

"Nope. All that land along the water is owned by Harriet Hooper," said Stella. "Plus it's sunny on this side, away from the woods."

Through the trees I caught glimpses of the covered bridge, the one Fin had shown me weeks ago. I considered telling Stella about it, but she couldn't seem to stop talking.

"Anyway," she said, "that's a long way of saying what it is I wanted to tell you."

I realized I hadn't heard a word she'd said. "Sorry, I missed that. What did you want to tell me?"

"You know, about Wyatt."

"What about Wyatt? Is he okay?"

"He's fine. It's just that, well, I guess I should come out and say it directly. He's not my nephew."

"He's not? Who is he?"

"Wyatt is my son."

Chapter 17

I stopped on the edge of the road and stared at her.

"I knew I should have told you from the beginning, Chloe. I feel so bad for lying about it."

I could feel myself breathing faster. Stella was a mom?

"Are you okay?" she asked. "Let's go to the beach and sit down, so I can tell you everything."

I forced myself to follow her as she rushed ahead. But my legs felt heavy, like they didn't want to move.

A couple minutes later, Stella turned left and plowed through a small parking lot where an ice cream truck played one of those irritating jingles in a loop. She waited for me to catch up, but I couldn't make myself go any faster.

A few people were sprawled out across a strip of sand that ran between some picnic tables and the river. Stella spread her towel off to the side, away from everyone else, so I did the same.

I watched as she arranged herself neatly, as an adult would do. The thought of hanging out with a person who was a mother seemed absurd to me, even embarrassing, but I was trapped.

"Remember when I mentioned that my mom left when I was little?" She twisted around and laid down on her stomach, as if settling in for a long afternoon. I picked up a stick and poked at the ground.

"Well, the truth is my mom had an addiction problem, and other problems, and eventually settled down in Florida. I've only seen her a few times since she took off. So my dad ended up remarrying and my stepmom is like, very religious—I mean super religious—and has all these rules. It was hard losing my mother like that, but even harder living with my stepmother. So hard."

I found it was easier to listen to Stella, and not freak out, if I doodled in the sand.

"That's why Dave left," she continued. "He was in high school when our dad married our stepmom, and he couldn't stand her from the moment she marched through the door and started ordering us around. Dave rebelled and ended up getting in a lot of trouble, so our stepmom kicked him out and he went to live with Birdie, who's our real mom's mother. I never really saw Birdie growing up, because my stepmother didn't let me visit her, but Birdie always sent presents and cards on my birthday. And I know she still sends money to my mom in Florida."

At this point, Stella took a deep breath and exhaled loudly.

"I don't want to bore you with all the details, Chloe, but I hope if I give you some background, it might be easier to understand why I lied to you."

All at once, I didn't want to do this. I didn't want to hear the story of her life or her grownup secrets. I just wanted to be a kid sitting by the water on a hot July day. Playing my own game. A harmless, silly game that would all be over at the end of the summer.

"Do you want to get ice cream now?" I jumped up and brushed sand off my feet. "I brought some money, so you don't have to pay for mine."

"What?" Stella twisted around and stared up at me, as if she didn't understand my question. "But I'm not done telling you about Wyatt."

My legs seemed to fold all on their own. I pulled my knees into my chest and dug my toes into the hole I'd created.

"Anyway, when I got older, my stepmom never allowed me to go to school dances," she continued, "because she claimed they were inappropriate for girls my age. But I really wanted to go to the Sophomore Dance with Rand Ramirez. After begging my stepmom and doing every chore imaginable, I finally wore her down and she let me go. Only she thought I was going with my best friend, Tiffy. But Tiffy was covering for me so I could actually go with Rand. Anyway, Rand and me, we never made it to the dance. And that night, I accidentally got myself pregnant with Wyatt."

This time, I stood up so fast you'd think I had red ants crawling up my legs.

"Well, it's nice of you to tell me," I said. "I'm gonna see if they have any of those ice pops. Do you want one? I love lemon ice pops."

Stella looked up again, her hand over her forehead to block out the sun. "Chloe, I'm still not done. I haven't told you the most important part."

I remained standing and crossed my arms, as if to brace myself for all the details I dreaded hearing.

"So I didn't even know I was pregnant for a really long time. I just thought I was gaining weight until I finally made a doctor's appointment. My stepmom almost died when she found out, and she definitely didn't want anyone from their church to know. At first, she and my dad were going to make me hide somewhere far away and give up my baby for adoption. But I told them I'd run away if they did that. So they decided to let me live with Birdie. The only thing was, it had to be permanent. My stepmother said they didn't want to have anything to do with me, or my baby, ever again."

After that, Stella was quiet. I wasn't sure if she was going to cry, so I sat down again and tried to think of something to say. "Birdie seems really nice."

Stella rubbed her eyes. "Birdie's the best grandmother in the whole world. She'd never turn away anyone in the family who needed help. Not like my dad did."

Something about Stella's story reminded me of Dot's. It occurred to me that a lot of people I knew had way worse problems than I did. Even though I didn't have my mother and father living together in one place, no one was trying to get rid of me.

"When I first moved here," said Stella, "I had a

hard time making friends at the high school, mostly because everyone knew I had a baby." She paused and rubbed her eyes some more. "Some people called me terrible names. It got so bad, Birdie let me stay home and take courses online. I got my GED last winter, which is the same as getting a high school diploma."

She glanced over at me and smiled a little.

"As soon as I met you, Chloe, someone new who didn't know anything about me, I decided to pretend I was just a teenager again. And not a mom. So we could be friends and I could maybe be friends with your sister. I don't know if all that makes sense, but Birdie finally convinced me it was wrong to do. And that I need to be true to my story and to never let other people write it."

A cloud passed overhead and darkened the beach. It was as if all the guilt I was feeling at that moment hovered above us.

"Most of all," she continued, "I was wrong by Wyatt, who I love more than anyone or anything in the entire world. I'm proud of him and I never want him to think I don't want to be his mother. So, that's it. That's my story."

Now I understood Birdie's hesitation when I'd brought up Wyatt's father. And why she'd told me

Stella needed a friend. Everything was starting to make sense once she told me the truth.

"There's something about you, Chloe, that makes me want to be a better person. You're so sensitive and caring and, I don't know, kind. I'm really sorry I lied to you and I hope you can forgive me."

I didn't know what to say. Everything about me was a lie.

Or was it?

I felt so confused. This game was supposed to be fun, but now it felt like some horrible trick that had twisted me into knots.

"I think you're great," I said finally, because at least that was the truth. "Wyatt is lucky to have you as his mom."

She gave me one of those too-big smiles that happens when you're really relieved. "See, that's what I mean—you're the sweetest. Hey, you've been so quiet listening to me blather on. How about I buy you one of those lemon ice pops now?" Stella stood up and stretched. "Or anything you want!"

But I couldn't move. I sat perfectly still and gazed across the river where the woods were thick.

"Are you coming?" she called as she jogged toward the parking lot.

Just then I noticed something move slowly through the trees. Big, like a large animal.

"One second," I called to Stella as I walked down to the water to get a better look. The animal paused and pushed its head through the branches into the light. Now I was sure that I wasn't imagining what I was seeing.

It was Fin riding Beryl.

Chapter 18

I barely remember eating my ice pop.

As we walked back along the road, Stella continued to talk. I tried to listen and respond to her here and there. But I couldn't stop thinking about Fin, wondering when he'd returned. Maybe there was something waiting for me at the farm stand.

As soon as we reached the bridge, I told Stella that I'd promised my dad I would pick up some vegetables for dinner.

"Your dad?" she exclaimed. "Does that mean your parents are back from camping?"

A slip. A big slip. I blamed it on being on the wrong side of the bridge. Everything felt so mixed up.

"Yesterday. They got back last night."

"Wow, that was a long trip. Well, now all four of you can come for dinner! Birdie will love that."

I stared at her joyful face and tried to think of something to say, but all I wanted to do was check the farm stand for a bag.

"Oh, and I forgot to tell *you* something," said Stella as we strolled across the bridge together. "That boy came in the store yesterday morning."

"Fin?"

"He wasn't strange at all this time." She paused and picked up a stone, then tossed it at the rushing water. "He actually said *hello* like a normal person, and smiled. I guess I was all wrong about him."

The sun was low. Looking at it filled me with sadness. Fin had been back for more than a whole day.

"Did he buy anything?" I don't know why I asked that, because it didn't matter.

"A quart of milk. That was it. And then he— Chloe, are you all right? You don't seem like yourself today."

I shook my head and tried not to tear up. "I'm fine. And then he what? What did he do after he bought the milk?"

"Well, he said *See ya round* as if he always said stuff like that. And then he left."

Everything I had assumed about my friend-ship with Fin now felt wrong. He didn't care that I thought about him almost all the time. Obviously, he didn't think about me at all.

Then Stella asked, "Have you two been hanging out?"

"Not really," I lied. I couldn't stop lying. Everything felt like a lie. As if the truth was the lie and the lie was the truth.

Stella hugged me. "Listen, I gotta run. Wyatt's probably asking for me back at the house. Thank you for an awesome day, Chloe, and for letting me unload without being all judgy like everyone else. Like I said before, you're the best. Tell that sister of yours I really have to meet her."

I kept nodding like one of those hollow bobble heads as I watched her rush to the other side of the bridge, past the *Welcome to Renew* sign and beyond the store, then around the corner and out of sight. In a way, it was like watching Chloe disappear.

xxx

Thank goodness for Tutu. She was waiting in the back hall by the door, sitting at attention with those perky ears. Her tiny tail swept the floor back and forth, as if she knew I needed her.

I bent down and held her close.

A note from Dad on the kitchen counter said he would be late tonight, and that dinner was in the refrigerator. I opened the door to look. A plate of spaghetti and a salad in a small bowl. I didn't feel like eating—I didn't feel like doing anything—so I left it there.

Normally, being by myself in this big house, like it was all mine and not Julia's, had been one of my favorite things about living here. For the first time in my life, the world wasn't crowded and complicated and noisy. It was uncluttered and simple and peaceful. But at that moment, being alone felt lonely. Because I couldn't stop thinking about Fin and why he didn't want to see me.

When my parents were going through the divorce, Viva would tell me to distract myself. She said there was nothing I could do to change what had happened, so it was best to not think about it. If only Viva were here now, I wouldn't need to be distracted. But she didn't want to see me either.

What was wrong with me? Why didn't anyone care about me? Maybe Dot and I were more alike than I'd realized. Two rejects.

I picked up Tutu and slowly climbed the stairs,

then collapsed against the pillows on my bed. She snuggled against my side. I reached over to the night table and dug my cell phone out of the drawer. It had been a long time since I'd checked it.

Rows and rows of messages from Mo appeared, and almost as many voicemails. I scrolled past them until I saw a new text from Megan, just a couple days old: *Summer without you isn't summer. When are you back?*

For a second, I wanted to call her, maybe even take the bus back to Kettleboro and forget I ever met Fin. But I texted instead.

Not sure.

Her reply came seconds later. *I'm really sorry about everything.*

I wanted to write back, but then I reminded myself that Megan was friends with Lux now. And every horrible thing Megan and the girls had said about me that night still stung. So I said nothing and continued to scroll.

The next message from Mo caught my eye. It began with the words, *It's about your sister . . .* I clicked on it to read the rest: *. . . Please call me asap!* Mo had sent it yesterday. My heart pounded as I sat up and pressed her number.

"Well howdy, stranger!"

I could hear a television blaring in the background.

"Mo! Is Viva okay?"

"What? Agnes? Wait. Let me go in the other room where it's quieter."

I groaned so loudly, Tutu moved away from me to the other end of the bed.

"Hello, Agnes? How's this? Can you hear me better? I'm outside on our deck now. You should see the view of the lake we have from the backyard!"

"I don't care about your backyard. What's wrong with Viva?"

"Who said anything is wrong with Viva? Oh! A cormorant just landed on the water. Or maybe it's a loon, hard to tell from here."

I knew Mo was narrating the wildlife activity as a way of telling me how wonderful their life was in Topeka. As if her bird report would somehow lure me to join them. But I also knew it meant she had nothing to tell me about Viva.

"Why did you text me about Viva and order me to call you *asap*?"

"Oh, that all happened yesterday," she said shouting even louder than usual. "I called to leave your sister a message, like I do every once in a while, even though she never calls back. Sound familiar? Anyway, this time when I called her, a recording came on saying her phone was no longer in service."

"What? Why?"

Viva's number was the only connection I had left to her, even though she never returned my messages either.

"I had no idea, and thought maybe you knew. But then Richard suggested I call our service provider, which was a brilliant idea. Turns out, Viva dropped out of our family plan completely and changed phone companies. But they couldn't give me any more details than that."

"Can she do that? Just drop her phone number?"

"She can if she wants to pay her own bill." Mo took a deep breath and added, "Richard thinks it may be that I called her one too many times."

Richard was probably right, but I wasn't about to admit that.

"So, Agnes? I won't keep bugging you either, honey. I just miss my girls and wish we were all together."

If only she knew how much I wished that too. If only everything could be the way it used to be.

Chapter 19

After promising Mo I would check in occasionally if she promised to stop leaving voicemails and texts on my phone five times a day, I collapsed onto my pillow again and took a deep breath. Tutu was already asleep by my feet.

The next thing I knew, someone was tapping at the door. I opened my eyes and couldn't figure out the time. It seemed as if only a few minutes had passed, but the room was filled with early morning sunshine. My clothes were still on, but I was under the covers.

I rolled over and looked for Tutu, but she was gone.

More tapping. "May I come in, Agnes?"

Unlike Mo, my dad didn't barge into every aspect of my life.

Something was caught under my knee. I reached in the covers and pulled out a book: *25 Best Bicycle*

Tours in Vermont. Now I remembered finding it on the bottom shelf of the nightstand and reading it before I fell asleep.

"Sure," I answered and sat up against the pillows.

The door opened slowly. Dad was holding Tutu with one hand, a glass of juice with his other. He sat on the edge of my bed as he placed Tutu in my arms.

"What time is it?" I asked.

"Almost nine o'clock. I've already been working for an hour."

"In the morning? How could I have slept that long?"

Dad reached over and stroked my hair. "I'm glad I didn't wake you last night. You were sound asleep when I spread the blanket and turned out your light."

I yawned and stretched.

"Reading another book?" he asked.

I handed it to him and he looked surprised.

"Your friend Julia must love bikes as much as we do," I said. "Have you seen how many she has in her barn?"

"Yes, I have," said Dad. He glanced down and took a long breath. "Listen, you should know that Julia is not just a friend, Agnes. She's a *very* good friend."

"Oh." I'd kind of suspected that, but I didn't want

to think about my dad having very good friends. Especially ones I'd never met.

"And she's the conductor of the Prelude Conservatory Orchestra," he added, as if that made a difference.

"Really? I thought conductors were always men."

"Of course conductors can be women too," he said and squeezed my nose, something he hadn't done since I was little. "Oops, looks like your nose fell off," he teased, showing me his thumb curled up between his fingers.

I couldn't help giggling. "Stop it, Dad."

He leaned over and kissed my cheek. "Nice to see you laugh. I feel like I haven't been paying enough attention to you lately, Agnes. Why didn't you eat your dinner last night?"

Instantly, Fin flooded my thoughts.

"I got stuck on an annoying call with Mo and forgot about the spaghetti," I replied, which wasn't entirely untrue. I rubbed my stomach and said, "But I'm starving now."

He patted my leg. "Good. How about waffles?"

"Waffles? Don't you need to get back to your office and work?"

"Not today. In fact, I have some wonderful news to tell you. Come on down when you're ready."

For a while I was able to forget everything that was weighing on me, even Fin. We ate waffles smothered in butter and maple syrup out on the front porch. Beyond the barn, mist floated above the field filled with purple wildflowers. Tutu slept peacefully on the rocking chair. It was a perfect moment that I wanted to hold onto forever.

"So are you going to tell me about your wonderful news?"

He finished chewing before wiping his chin with a napkin. Then pushed his chair back and smiled with his whole face. "I turned in my dissertation this morning."

"Your what?"

"The big paper! The one I've been working on for *years*."

"You mean you're done? You have your PhD now?"

He shook his head as he took a long sip of coffee. "Almost. After it's approved, I'll have to defend it. Which means I have to answer a bunch of questions about the big paper. But *then* I'll have my PhD."

"So does that mean you don't have to work upstairs in the office anymore? You have the rest of the summer off?"

"I wish," he said. "Fall classes start in a month, so I have a lot of prep to do. Plus I have to focus on my cello and catch up on weeks of serious practicing."

Somehow his cello always spoiled everything.

"But today, I'm all yours!" Dad added. "I think I've earned a day off and I owe you some quality time. What do you say we take a bike ride? I know a great ten-mile loop that I bet isn't in that book."

I couldn't think of a better way to spend the day. I finished my last waffle and told him I'd be ready in fifteen minutes.

"I just have one little favor I need to ask, Agnes."

"You mean other than walk the dog before we go?"

Tutu heard me and stood up on the rocking chair, her tail wagging.

Dad grinned. "I have to attend an important dinner party tonight."

"Oh, okay. We can be home by—"

"At Roger's house," he said, before I could finish. "And it would be nice if you could keep Dot company."

I slumped down in my seat. "Daaadddd. You've ruined a perfectly amazing day."

"Oh come on, Dot's not that bad."

I crossed my arms. "Then *you* hang out with her."

He picked up my plate, still sticky with syrup, and placed it on top of his. "It won't be just the two of you anyway."

"What does that mean?"

I followed him inside to get the dog leash.

"Roger and I are meeting with a very wealthy couple, potential donors who may give a sizeable donation for a new performance hall, and their daughter will be there as well. Apparently she's the same age as you and Dot."

That sounded even worse. I whined as loudly as I could to make my position clear.

"If you do this favor for me, Agnes, I *promise* I'll owe you a bigger favor in return."

I thought about that for a second. "How big?"

"Anything," he said, "within reason, of course."

×××

Biking with Dad washed away the last year of divorce world. I almost believed life could go back to feeling normal again.

We rode the opposite direction of my usual route, down roads I hadn't explored. At first, ten miles sounded way too far to ride a bike. But when Dad told me we were almost halfway, it felt as if we'd just left the house.

Up ahead, a line of wild turkeys blocked the road. They squawked and flapped their clumsy wings as we coasted toward them, waiting for them to cross.

A few minutes later Dad pointed with his right arm, the signal for making a turn in traffic, even though we hadn't passed anyone other than the turkeys. Our bikes rattled as we rode over a wooden bridge that crossed the river.

The next part of the loop was hilly, and my legs started to ache. Dad slowed down and rode next to me. "You've become quite the cyclist, Agnes!"

All at once, my legs felt stronger and I pedaled as hard as I could.

At the top of a steep hill, Dad pulled off to the side. "I need a break," he said, but I knew he was stopping for me.

We both took sips from our water bottles and gazed out at the view of the valley below. Off to the left, a cluster of buildings and streets rose out of the miles of fields.

"Is that the college?" I asked.

"It is, and way in the distance you can see Lake Champlain and Burlington."

There was a pause and I knew we were both thinking about Viva. How perfect this day would have been if she were riding with us.

Dad's voice perked up. "And see, there's the river directly below. We've almost made a full loop. Our house is right around the corner on the other side of Renew. In fact, it's all downhill from here to the stone bridge."

The back of my neck tensed. "We're in Renew?"

"That's how loops work," he said motioning with his finger, "one big circle."

The possibility of running into anyone I knew was practically zero, but I couldn't help feeling nervous. What if Stella was outside sweeping the front steps of the store? Or, worse, Fin was stocking the farm stand?

As we soared down the long slope, I kept my head low and positioned myself directly behind my dad. Our speed picked up and we rode so fast I was convinced we would safely fly by everything . . . until we rounded the last corner and Birdie's shot into view. Dad braked so hard I had to swerve to avoid crashing into him.

"Sorry about that," he said as he pulled over in front of the store. "I just remembered I wanted to pick up a few things and see if they have a menu."

The trees seemed to be closing in on me as the wind swirled in circles. I forced myself to calm down. Luckily, no one was in sight. I had a few seconds to gather my thoughts.

"Dad, I really need to get back to the house, if you know what I mean," I said, not even sure what I was implying, other than something urgent and personal.

But he leaned his bike against a tree anyway and walked toward the door. My heart skipped a beat as he peered through the window.

"It will only take a minute," he said and reached for the handle.

"Okay, well—I'll meet you back home!"

I turned my bike around before he could respond. But not before something caught my eye across the street. A paper bag sitting on the end of the farm stand, next to a big basket of cucumbers.

I wanted more than anything to race across and peer inside the bag, but I knew I had to get away from there as fast as I could.

Chapter 20

We arrived at Roger and Dot's house fifteen minutes late, because Dad had to take a last-minute call. His voice changed after he answered it.

"I'll meet you in the car, Agnes," he said as he ran up the stairs to his office with his phone in his hand. "This will only take a few seconds."

Even though the sun had set behind the trees, the car was still hot. So I leaned against the old maple tree and waited. For a second, I considered jumping on my bike and racing over to the farm stand to get the bag. Part of me was dying to know why Fin had been hiding from me the last few days. But another part of me felt I should pretend to not care, so he wouldn't know how much I liked him.

"Was that Mo?" I asked as Dad rushed through the front door wrapping a tie around his neck.

I couldn't remember the last time I'd seen my dad dressed up.

"Hm?" he replied. We climbed in the green sports car and rolled down the windows.

"On the phone? Who was that?"

"Oh, it was Julia checking on the house."

"Then why did you have to go upstairs to talk to her?"

He made a grumbly noise as he shifted the car. "Always tricky to get the gears in reverse," he said instead of answering me, then sped off down the road.

The reminder that we didn't own the house or the car or any of this, and that the summer would soon turn into fall, suddenly made me sad. The river and woods rushed by as I pressed my face against the window. Everything felt like a blur. I didn't want this life to end, but I didn't know how to keep it going.

"Timothy and Agnes! What a relief to see you both."

Roger stood in the doorway wearing a suit similar to Dad's. I wondered if I should have dressed up more than my usual denim shorts and flip-flops.

"Are they here yet?" asked Dad.

Roger nodded. "Seventeen minutes ago." We followed him down a long hallway. The house was huge and old-fashioned, full of dark antique furniture.

"Sorry to be late," said Dad, "but Julia phoned to check on the fall plans."

"I thought you said she was checking on the house?" I asked.

Both men stopped and stared at me like they didn't know what I was talking about.

"Yes, the house too," Dad said quickly, and then, "So where's Dot? Agnes has been looking forward to seeing her."

I didn't know why he felt he had to say that, since he knew I couldn't stand her.

Roger beamed. "She's downstairs in the family room, Agnes, entertaining our special young guest, and I know they can't wait to see you too. We'll be in the living room with the grown-ups until dinner."

He spoke to me carefully and slowly as if he were explaining something to a five-year-old kid. No wonder Dot acted so much younger than she was.

"Hello there, *Chloe*," said Dot as soon as I stepped through the door.

I quickly scanned the room, but no one else was there. "Don't call me that, Dot!"

"I'm not Dot. *Vladlena*, remember?"

She was sitting on a leather couch next to a fluffy yellow cat. Her pale legs weren't long enough to reach the floor, so they stuck out like two toothpicks from the bottom of her dress.

I dropped down next to her and stroked the cat. "I'm not calling you Vladlena either. You're Dot and I'm Agnes. Got it?"

"But you said it was okay when it was just the two of us."

"Well, it's not anymore, so forget I ever told you."

Her lips folded in, like she was either sad or mad.

I couldn't believe I'd ever felt sorry for Dot and confessed to her about Chloe and let her think we could be friends. What was I thinking? I had my own problems to worry about.

"So how long have you had your cat?" I asked, to get her mind off Chloe.

"It's not mine, I'm allergic to them," Dot mumbled and held up her nose spray. "That girl brought it."

The cat was so soft and calm I picked her up and placed her on my legs. The way she vibrated when she purred tickled my skin.

"You mean the special guest we're supposed to entertain? Where is she anyway?"

"In the bathroom. And she won't like you holding Madrid, because she told me not to touch her."

"Madrid, like the city in Spain?"

Just then, a small side door opened.

"Oh. My. God. Is that *you*, Agnes Moon?"

I couldn't believe it. Standing in front of me was my worst nightmare.

Madrid's claws dug into my thighs as she leapt from my lap and sprinted across the carpet. I blinked over and over, hoping I was hallucinating.

Lux Lockhart? Lux's parents were the wealthy donors?

She scooped up her cat and pressed her cheek against its furry head.

"Do you two know each other?" asked Dot.

Neither of us responded.

Dot tried again. "Do you live in the same town?"

Lux dropped down into a chair, still holding the cat, and smiled in a strange way.

"Megan thought you were kidnapped or something," she said, still gazing down at her cat. "We didn't know what happened to you until we'd heard you'd left town. Wait until I tell her I found you."

Dot stared at me, her mouth hanging open, as if I

really had been kidnapped. But I couldn't speak, the same way I couldn't speak at the sleepover.

"I thought I told you that no one was to touch my cat," added Lux, now addressing Dot.

Dot began to say something, but then stopped herself and looked down at the floor.

"Dinner, girls!" Roger burst into the room and clapped his hands together. "Everything's served! But why don't we leave Madrid in the kitchen or somewhere cozy while we eat?"

Lux stood up. "She'll be fine with me."

Then she strolled across the room and pushed past Roger, who exclaimed, "Excellent!" and followed her up the stairs without saying anything more to us.

Dot shook her head. "That has to be the meanest girl I've ever met."

And just like that, Dot didn't seem so bad anymore.

xxx

The seven of us, plus the cat, sat at a long dining room table under a fancy chandelier. I grabbed the seat farthest from Lux on the opposite side. My stomach was in knots. I knew Dad really wanted this performance hall, but he had no idea the donors' daughter had destroyed my life.

As the food moved around the table, the adults discussed the boring cello music playing in the background, some famous student they were still hoping to bring to the college. Dot, who was stuck sitting next to Lux, quietly picked at her food as if she'd rather be anywhere else than here. Lux stared down at either her phone or her cat in her lap, ignoring all of us. So for a few minutes, I was hopeful no one would find out that we actually knew each other.

Then Dad had to ask, "Where do you go to school, Lux?"

I dropped my fork and it banged against my plate.

Without looking up, Lux mumbled, "Pico."

Dad did a double-take, glancing back and forth between us. "Did you say Pico? That's where Agnes goes!"

"I knew it," said Dot.

I shot a silent warning at her and she didn't say another word.

Roger chimed in. "What a lovely coincidence. I thought you folks lived in Wentworth?"

"We do," said Lux's stepfather, who resembled a bulldog with a tuft of gray hair, "but we're part of some regional system where children from different towns are forced to go to school with each other."

"To be honest," said her mother, who was pointy all over, "we've never had to deal with public schools. But Lux wasn't admitted to either of the day academies in the region, and she refuses to board, so we had no choice."

Lux didn't get into private school? I glanced over at her and could see she was scowling more than usual. It was pretty awful of her mother to say that in front of everyone, and I began to wonder if Lux's life wasn't as fantastic as she pretended it was.

"The public schools aren't so bad," said Dad, then winked at me, letting me know he thought that the Lockharts were snobs. "They've served my daughters well. Wouldn't you agree, Roger?"

"To each his own," said Roger as he dabbed his mouth with the cloth napkin. "Speaking of schools, if we want to attract students at the level of this gifted cellist we're listening to, von Zimmermann, we really need to build a state-of-the-art facility to bring in the cream of the crop. And we would love nothing more than to be able to call it the Lockhart Performing Arts Center. That is if you both—"

At that moment, Lux interrupted Roger and

spoke directly to my dad. "I met Agnes through my best friend, Megan. But we don't really know each other since we've only hung out once."

Dot was right. Lux was the meanest girl in the entire world.

"That's funny," said Dad, "because Agnes's best friend is also named—"

He paused as soon as he saw my expression.

"She says hi, by the way," Lux added, holding up her phone.

I couldn't believe it. Lux was messaging Megan right in front of me.

"We aren't allowed to have our phones at the dinner table," said Dot, almost as if she was sticking up for me.

Roger laughed nervously. "Of course, we can make an exception for a very special guest!"

Throughout the rest of the meal, including dessert, I refused to look up from my plate. The minutes felt like hours as the adults droned on and on.

Finally, Dad slid his chair back.

"I'm so sorry, you'll have to excuse us," he said. "Agnes wasn't feeling well earlier and I can see she really should be home resting. I hate to leave, everyone, but I think we have to call it a night."

I slipped out of the room, without saying anything to anyone, before Dad finished his goodbyes.

Dot caught up to me as I opened the front door. "No one was messaging her," she whispered. "I saw her phone the whole time."

"You did?"

"She was looking at clothes."

I felt my lips curl, though I was still too upset to really smile. "Thanks, Dot."

"For what?"

"I guess, for being you."

The adults' voices grew louder as they headed toward us down the hall. Before Dot could respond, I quickly closed the door behind me.

Chapter 21

"You seem very upset, honey."

Dad drove extremely slowly back to the house, as if I might break in half if he hit a bump too hard. I refused to answer.

"I hope you know you can always tell me if something is bothering you."

I crossed my arms and focused on the world outside. On the trees and meadows and the winding river as we followed it for miles back to a house that wasn't ours. That would never be ours. I wished, more than anything, that I could live on the other side of the stone bridge as Chloe forever.

"Listen, I know something's wrong, Agnes, but I'm afraid this donation is a big deal. And the Lockharts are the only donors so far to come forward with major funding. So I need to understand if something happened between you and their daughter."

It was as if a spark, deep inside of me, ignited and set off an explosion.

"*Why*? So you can get money for your precious building even if it means begging the obnoxious parents of the most evil human being on the planet?"

Dad pulled into the driveway and turned off the car. It was pitch dark outside under a tent of clouds. No stars or moonlight.

He rubbed his forehead and said, "I know kids can be cruel."

"So can adults."

I slammed the car door behind me and stomped off toward the porch. The whole disastrous dinner and reminders of that humiliating sleepover and losing Megan and every single terrible thing that had ever happened since the divorce surged into a sharp, painful focus.

I wanted to pick up a rock and hurl it at the house. I wanted to hurl a whole bunch of rocks.

"Agnes, wait. You're being impossible." Dad slammed his car door too. "In fact, it's been impossible to talk to you about anything since you've arrived."

I whipped around. "Because you and Mo have made my whole life *impossible* to live!"

He froze. "What's that supposed to mean?"

"It means that ever since you and your cello walked out on us, everything has fallen apart! Mo immediately downloaded that disgusting dating app and met the weirdest person in the world and his even weirder son and cares a hundred more times about them than she does about me, and then Viva completely stopped talking to any of us and doesn't care at all about me anymore, and the one best friend I've had since I was four years old dumped me for a spoiled rich brat named *Luxembourg Lockhart* whose favorite hobby is to ruin other people's lives!"

I collapsed into a heap onto the bottom step of the porch and burst into tears. A tidal wave of emotions engulfed my entire body, and I couldn't stop sobbing.

I felt my dad sit next to me, and I moved to the other end of the step.

"Oh Agnes. I didn't walk out on you and Viva. In fact, I didn't want to leave at all and hoped we could somehow figure out to how to continue as a family under one roof. But it wasn't realistic. Your mother and I needed the space from each other to get on with our lives."

"Leaving us was the worst possible thing you could have done," I yelled into my chest, still curled over in a ball.

My dad moved toward me again and touched my back. "I know it's hard to believe, Agnes, but I've been trying to do my best with the situation. It breaks my heart to hear all of this. I already feel so cut off from Viva. It would devastate me if I lost you too. You girls are the most important people in the world to me."

I sat up and wiped my nose with the back of my hand. "We are?"

He wrapped both arms around me and pulled me close. "How can you not know that?"

"Because everyone and everything seems to matter more to you. Your students, the college, this town, *your cello*. You left our life and chose this life."

"That's not true. This wasn't a choice I wanted to make. I couldn't afford to live anywhere else and still support you kids. But now that my dissertation is done and my PhD is in sight, things will be much better. You can visit more often, and maybe Viva will too someday."

"I don't want to visit you anymore," I said.

Dad's face fell. "You don't?"

"I want to live with you."

He dropped one arm away from me, leaving the other arm draped over my shoulder.

"You promised me this morning that if I went to Roger's dinner party you would owe me a big favor. This is the favor I want."

The wind picked up and flashes of silent lightning lit the dark clouds. Dad stared up at the sky.

"Okay," he said quietly.

I was so used to disappointment and rejection that I wasn't sure if I'd understood him.

"Okay what?"

He kissed the top of my head. "Okay, you can live with me."

My heart immediately began to race. I tried to catch my breath. "I can? But I thought I had to live with Mo."

"I've been assuming that was best for you, Agnes, but now I can see things are more complicated than that. I'll have to discuss it with your mother, of course, but we'll work it out. I promise."

I jumped up and shrieked so loudly that Tutu began barking from inside the house. A clap of thunder cracked open the nighttime sky. I threw my arms around Dad and we hugged each other as the clear, cool rain poured down on us.

xxx

It's amazing how one day your life can be a catastrophe, and then the next day you're on top of the world.

In the morning, I took my time riding over to the farm stand. For some reason, I no longer felt upset with Fin. And I was positive the contents of the bag would explain everything. I had my dad back and nothing else mattered. Finally, my life was falling into place.

Even though the sun was still behind the trees, it was already hot and the heat bugs were buzzing in the bushes. A perfect summer day.

Because of the storm the night before, the river rushed higher than usual. I paused midway across the bridge and took in the watery rainbow, which still arched between the rocks when you tilted your head just so.

After passing the *Welcome to Renew* sign and rounding the corner, I stopped, like always, to twist my hair back into a bun. And become Chloe. But this time I hesitated, wondering how I could continue this game once I was living here permanently with my dad.

The warm scent of sugary donuts filled the air outside Birdie's. I wanted to burst into the store and share my great news with Stella, but then that would mean telling her everything. And I didn't know how. It was something I needed to figure out sooner rather than later, but for now, I would enjoy myself and worry about it later.

I couldn't guess what I would find inside the paper bag at the farm stand this time, but I assumed it would still be there. When it wasn't, I searched for it under and between every basket of vegetables, and then checked the ground. Fin must have taken it back.

I decided to ride my bike down to the farm and find out exactly what was going on with him. As I got closer to the fork in the road I noticed the *Wing Repairs* sign missing from the tree. I parked my bike and walked the rest of the way.

Peering around one of the stone gate posts at the entrance of the farm, I saw Fin standing in the back of an old pickup truck. He was dropping empty cages down to Harriet, who set them on the ground.

After watching the two of them work together for a minute, I noticed they weren't talking to each other.

"Hi!" I waved and walked toward them.

They both glanced in my direction, but then Fin immediately looked away.

"Chloe," said Harriet, "it's good to see you."

Hearing her call me Chloe suddenly felt wrong, almost shameful, as if I'd stolen something from her.

She met me halfway and gave me a hug. I glanced past her at Fin, who appeared to be ignoring me.

"Don't mind him," she whispered. "We released our last patient today, so he's feeling a little blue."

"The hawk or the falcon?" I asked.

"Both. The hawk first, and then the falcon, who seemed reluctant to go. We stayed up there for a couple hours with her, but she didn't move from her perch. So we let her be. We just got back from the mountain."

Harriet nodded in Fin's direction and whispered a little more softly. "I had to close up shop, even though he didn't want me to. He could use some cheering up."

Now I felt a little sad too. I had been looking forward to watching at least one of the raptors take off, but somehow I'd missed my chance.

As Harriet climbed the hill to the house, I made my way over to the side of the truck. I watched as Fin wound a long piece of rope around his arm.

"I saw you," I said, "riding Beryl."

Finally, he looked at me. "When?"

"A couple of days ago. In the woods across from the town beach."

The way his body shifted, I could tell he didn't expect to hear that. He brushed his hands and dropped down off the back of the truck.

"You would have known that if you'd bothered to read my note."

"What note?"

"The one I left in the bag at the farm stand a week ago."

"A week ago? But I didn't see the bag until yesterday."

"So why didn't you take it yesterday?"

There was no way to explain what had been going on with my dad, even though I wanted to tell him.

"I couldn't, but I checked the farm stand every day before that and didn't see it."

"It was there," he said. "You didn't look hard enough."

"Did you hide it?"

"I wedged it between the buckets of flowers and thought you'd find it," he said, his eyes narrowing. "I finally moved it to a more obvious spot, but then last night's rain ruined the bag."

He kicked at the ground.

"What was in it?"

"It doesn't matter anymore."

"It does to me." I said. "I've been freaking out knowing that you've been here and—"

I stopped myself from saying anymore. I didn't want him to know how much I'd been thinking about him. But it was too late. His lips had spread into a tiny smile.

"Stones."

"Stones?"

"Eight stones were in the bag. Actually, they were more like pebbles."

I waited for him to explain what was so special and important about eight stones. But then, as usual, he went in a completely different direction.

"Do you want to see where we released the birds?"

Chapter 22

We followed a grassy road that wound through the farm and up the steep hill behind Harriet's house. Neither of us said much as we walked, but every couple of minutes Fin bent down to pick up a rock and put it in his pocket. "What are those for?" I asked.

"You'll see."

Eventually the grassy road ended and became a worn footpath.

"The hawk was released over there on that tree," he said, pointing at the woods. "He took off pretty fast. Then I parked the truck and we carried the falcon all the way to the top."

"You know how to drive?" I asked.

"I got my learner's permit a few months ago."

Now Fin seemed even older than he already was. And I felt younger.

"So why isn't Harriet helping out with the raptors anymore?"

"She said she needs a break to take care of her own broken wings."

That seemed like a funny answer, but in a way, I understood. Maybe Harriet felt kind of the way I'd felt when Stella had told me about her past—sort of lost and overwhelmed. It was hard to help others if you hadn't figured out how to help yourself.

The trees cleared at the top of the hill with a wide view of the valley, almost the same view I had seen with my Dad on the bike ride. We stepped onto the rocky edge.

Fin hesitated and put a finger to his lips. With his other hand he silently pointed at a bird perched on a boulder.

"The falcon," he whispered. "She's still there in the exact same place."

"Is that a big deal?" I asked, speaking as softly as I could.

"They almost always fly away, or at least move, after a few hours."

The bird twitched and turned, as if she couldn't make a decision.

"Where do they go?"

"Back to their natural habitat, which, according to Harriet, is wherever they feel they belong." Then he looked at me and added, "She thinks everyone does eventually."

I thought about that for a few seconds. "Well, maybe this one doesn't know where she belongs."

At that moment, the bird puffed up her beautiful feathers, extended her wings, and took off . . . almost as if she'd heard us. We moved even closer to the edge and watched as she floated over the treetops, across the river, and down through the valley, winding back and forth, until she disappeared from sight. Fin was right. It was incredible to watch.

"Hopefully she'll figure it out," said Fin.

He sat down on a large smooth boulder and let his legs dangle over the side of the hill.

"Ready to play?" he asked, abruptly changing the subject.

I peered over the ledge. The drop-off wasn't as steep as it appeared, so I sat down next to him. "Play what?"

"Truth Stones." He pulled the rocks out of his pocket and handed four to me.

The name of the game worried me. For a second, I wondered if Fin knew I had been playing an opposite game. "How does it work?"

"We each get four stones. When it's your turn, you get to ask me anything and I have to answer truthfully. If I decide I can't answer truthfully, I have to give you one stone. If I answer truthfully, you have to give me a stone. Then it's my turn to ask you a question."

"But how do we know if the other person is answering truthfully?"

Fin tilted his head like he was confused. "Because we trust each other to be honest?"

I nodded and smiled, but inside, a tide of guilt surged through me. It was the same feeling I got earlier when Harriet called me Chloe.

"The one rule is you can't ask a question that's already been asked. Okay?"

"Okay. So how long do we play?"

"Until someone has all eight stones."

That sounded easy enough, especially since I didn't have to answer anything I didn't want to.

"You go first," he said.

"Hm . . ." I paused, trying to figure out what to ask. "What's your favorite dessert?"

He closed his eyes and rubbed his chin. "If I had to choose, I would say two scoops of cinnamon gelato from Fantasia's in Rome."

"Rome, *Italy*?"

He shook his head. "That's two questions. My turn and a stone please."

I was so surprised to hear that he'd traveled to Europe that I didn't hear his question.

"Well? Have you?" he said.

"Have I what?"

"You know, ever had a boyfriend?"

I didn't realize he was going to ask those kinds of questions.

"Of course I have," I replied. "I've had lots of friends who were boys."

He rolled his eyes. "You know that wasn't the question."

I frowned, then handed him a stone.

"What's your favorite sport?" I asked.

"Another favorite question? Don't you want to know anything more personal about me?"

At that point, I didn't want to play this game at all. It occured to me that the questions a fifteen-year-old would ask were very different from the things a twelve-year-old would want to know.

"This game isn't really fair," I said.

"It's completely fair if you open up and tell the truth."

My chest began to pound a little. "Okay then. Why do you have that scar?"

"Now you're playing!" He grinned. "Because I fell out of a tree when I was five years old and cracked my collarbone."

"Really? Is it okay now?"

I don't know why I'd assumed his scar had to be more serious than that. There was something about Fin that seemed so mysterious, but maybe he was just an ordinary person like everyone else.

"No follow-up questions." He took a stone from my hand, leaving me with one. "My turn."

All at once I had a bunch of things to ask, and didn't want the game to end. But I knew I had to answer truthfully if I wanted to get another chance.

"Where is your house?"

Again I tensed up. I was pretty sure he didn't mean Kansas, which wasn't the truth anyway.

"I already told you." I chose my words carefully. "On the other side of the river in Bittersweet."

"Shoot!" he handed me a stone. "I meant to ask the address."

I was thankful he hadn't.

The two stones in my fist now felt like hidden treasures. "Where do you go when you go away?"

He took so long to respond, I was sure he would give me one of his stones instead of answering.

"I go home to Canada," he finally replied, "to be with my family."

Now my head was spinning with questions. I handed him a stone. Only one left again and it was his turn.

He glanced at me out of the corners of his eyes. "Have you ever kissed anyone? I mean really kissed someone?"

Why was it so much harder to admit the truth than make something up?

I gritted my teeth. "No."

"See, that wasn't so bad," he said. His face was still serious, but his voice sounded more relaxed. Then he handed me a stone.

I was back up to two again.

"So if your family is in Canada," I asked, "why did you move in with Harriet?"

His whole face dropped and he didn't say anything for a few seconds.

"She's my birth mother," he replied. "I was adopted right after I was born by my parents, who, for various reasons, moved to Montreal when I was little. About a year ago, Harriet and I connected and she invited me to stay with her. I thought it would be for a month or so, but I'm still here."

His birth mother? Harriet didn't look old enough to be anyone's mother. But that explained the resemblance between them.

"My turn," he announced, clearly wanting to change the subject. "Why is your hair always pulled back?"

That question was the worst one yet. It had so many possible answers, and I didn't want to confess any of them. Then I thought about everything Fin had shared. About his scar, his home, Harriet.

"Mostly because I hate my hair."

"Why? The color is so unique. Somewhere between ginger and curry."

I didn't know what to say to that so I just shook my head, hoping I wasn't blushing. "Okay, whatever. It's my turn. If you could change only one thing about yourself," I asked, "what would it be?"

"Not my hair," he said. "I love my hair."

I laughed. "So what then?"

All of a sudden, his expression changed and he groaned.

"Sorry," I said quickly. "I can ask a different question."

"No, the rules are the rules," he said, then leaned back on his elbows and stared at the sky.

"But you don't have to answer if you don't want to."

"Actually, I do want to. I just need to find the right words."

I waited, having no clue what to expect. Tiny pieces of grass lined a crack in the rock. Fin reached over and pulled them out one at a time. I studied his hands, which were wide and large. Like my father's hands. I had never noticed that before.

Eventually, he smiled and turned his head toward me. "If I could change only one thing about myself, it would be my gender assignment when I was born."

I didn't understand that answer and wondered if had something to do with being adopted. "What do you mean?"

He took a long breath and exhaled slowly. "You were probably recognized as a female baby immediately at birth, right?"

"Of course," I said.

"Not of course," he corrected me, now sounding a little annoyed.

"I don't get it. What are you talking about?"

He squeezed the back of his neck. "Not every-one is easily determined male or female when they're born."

"They aren't?"

"Nope, they aren't." He said it so matter-of-factly that I felt embarrassed. Maybe this was something I would learn in middle school health class. Or in that book Mo had left me. Or on the internet that everybody but me could access with their smartphones.

"Some people are born somewhere in between. And that's what happened to me."

"Are you saying you weren't a boy when you were born?"

He gazed directly into my eyes. "I'm saying I wasn't clearly one or the other. At least not within society's narrow definition of genders, which says you have to look and feel all male or all female."

We were both silent for a minute. And then I had to ask, "So what happened?"

We had stopped trading stones several questions earlier, so I wasn't sure if the game had ended. But I figured that was the point of the game, to get to a place where you didn't need the stones anymore.

"Well, since they weren't exactly sure what I was,

they decided to wave their magic medical wand and give me female parts and make me a girl. Because no one likes ambiguity, especially in teeny tiny babies. But I'm not a girl. They made a mistake."

"Who did?"

"Everyone. The doctors. The nurses. The *experts.*"

I didn't know that a doctor could make that kind of mistake. "Did Harriet know?"

"Harriet saw me only briefly before my parents adopted me, and she was told I was a girl."

"Then what about your parents?"

"At first, they believed that the doctors knew best and didn't question their decision. Not until I began to walk and talk and call myself a boy. Apparently, when anyone referred to me as a girl, I pointed at myself in a mirror and said, boy. Sometimes I even got mad and hit the mirror. So eventually my parents worried that a mistake had been made. A big mistake. Then a psychologist and more experts confirmed the big mistake. So not long after that, everyone stopped calling me Abigail."

I didn't know what to say, or what I was supposed to say. So I said the first thing that came into my head. "You look like a boy."

He swallowed hard and made himself smile. "Well, I *am* a boy."

It occurred to me that I had never thought about being a girl. I just knew I was a girl. I couldn't imagine what it would be like to question that about yourself. In a way, though, I understood that feeling of not being recognized for who you were, no matter how hard people tried to label you, and it made me like him even more.

Fin leaned over and nudged me with his shoulder. "Thanks, by the way," he said.

"For what?"

"For not jumping up and running away screaming."

Running away hadn't crossed my mind. All I could think about was the long list of people who had let Fin down through the years, even when he was a baby.

"I would never do that to you. To me, you're just my friend, Fin."

"And you're just my friend, Chloe."

My heart sank. If there was ever a perfect moment for me to come clean, this would have been it. But I couldn't. This was Fin's moment. And compared to what had happened to him, nothing I could explain about Agnes's life would seem like that big of a deal. It certainly wouldn't seem bad enough to change my name and my identity. Two things he had to do. If I confessed now—admitting that Chloe was only a figment of my imagination to make others like me, so I would feel better about myself—I would seem so silly, so childish.

So . . . selfish.

Chapter 23

We didn't say much on the walk down. I had no
idea what Fin was thinking, but I felt changed, with
gusts of guilt blowing all around me. Fin had shared
personal and painful and complicated things about
himself. What excuse did I have for not even telling
him my real name?

Near the bottom of the hill, I spotted Beryl grazing next to the chickens, and two geese seemed to be
arguing over by the beehives.

Harriet stood on the porch, wearing a pale blue
dress. "Did you two have a pleasant stroll?"

"The falcon was still there," said Fin, "but she
finally took off."

"It can be hard to find your way home," said
Harriet. "Happens to a lot of us."

For the first time, I noticed lines around her eyes

and mouth, signs of being a grown-up with grown-up problems.

"Stay for lunch, Chloe?"

I wasn't really hungry, and I could tell Fin wanted to be alone. "I can't, but thanks."

He walked with me through the gate posts and down the dirt road, where my bike was leaning against the tree.

"I'm taking off tonight," he said, "but I'll be back this weekend."

I was disappointed to hear he was leaving again already, especially since I hadn't seen him in over a week. And I really wanted to tell him everything as soon as possible.

"At least I'll know where you'll be this time," I said. "Home in Canada."

"Actually, this is a different trip." He raised his eyebrows mysteriously. "I don't want to jinx it by talking about it, so I'll explain when I get back."

"More surprises?"

He flashed me a grin and said, "I'm full of surprises."

I nodded. And then, without giving it a second thought, I reached behind my head and untied my hair. The pile of copper coils exploded like streamers across my back. "So am I."

Fin gasped, "Whoa!"

I winced. "Good whoa or bad whoa?"

"Great whoa. Not that you weren't great whoa before. This is just a more enhanced whoa."

I laughed, then swung my leg over my bike seat and pushed off. "Enjoy wherever it is you're going!"

I glanced back one last time. Fin was still staring as my hair flew behind me. His first introduction to Agnes had gone well. Maybe if I revealed myself slowly, one layer at a time, everything would work out fine.

The sun glowed overhead as I pedaled up the dirt road. A calmness came over me. It was a relief to know I could stop pretending. For the first time in my life, I felt okay being Agnes. After all that Fin had been through in his life, I knew he would understand why I'd kept some secrets.

As I reached the end of the road, I saw Stella in front of the store. She was holding a spray bottle and cleaning the windows with a cloth.

I braked and straddled the center bar of my bike. "Looking good," I called across the street.

She turned and smiled. Then did a double take. "Wow! You have hair!" She rushed over. "Why were you hiding it? It's spectacular!"

Her eyes seemed to double in size through her thick glasses.

"Oh, you know, the summer heat and bugs. It's easier when it's up." But since that was only a small part of the truth, I added, "And I've never liked my hair. It's not, you know, smooth and silky like it's supposed to be."

"Who said hair is supposed to be smooth and silky? And do you know how many people spend hundreds of dollars trying to get that color?"

Stella always said exactly the right thing.

"Come on in for a few minutes. We have a bunch of leftover donuts that Birdie made for the Bingo tournament this morning. You should take some home."

As soon as she mentioned food, my stomach felt queasy, like I was really coming down with something. "Thanks, but I need to get going."

"Hey, how's your sister?" she called as I rode off toward the bridge. "Is she better yet?"

I twisted back in my seat and answered truthfully. "I'm not sure, but I'll let you know when I find out."

This was already going so much better than I thought it would. Confessing everything to Stella would be as easy as telling Fin. I just had to find the right time to do it.

Tutu didn't greet me when I opened the back door, although her little tail wagged as I passed her bed. I figured she was tired because Dad had already taken her for a walk.

Now that he'd finished his dissertation, Dad said he needed to spend more time on campus practicing his cello and getting ready for fall classes. We hadn't talked any more about living together, since there were so many details to work out first. Like convincing Mo. And, of course, we'd have to find a place to live, unless Julia wanted us to keep housesitting and taking care of Tutu forever, which would be fine with me.

A note was on the kitchen counter: *Having a party on Saturday to celebrate the thesis and more! Just a few people, including a special guest or two. Shopping for supplies on my way home. Text if you need me to pick up anything.*

I figured a party could be fun, though I wasn't sure what Dad was celebrating other than finishing his paper. I hoped the few people he was referring to didn't include Dot, but I had a feeling it did since Roger seemed to be one of my Dad's closest friends.

Now that I thought about it, the special guests were probably other boring musicians from the college.

All through supper that night, Dad was secretive about his party. He grinned like a little kid when I mentioned it, as if he was thinking of renting a pony or offering hot air balloon rides in the backyard.

I started with a basic line of questioning: "So what time does the big event start?"

"I asked everyone to arrive between five-thirty and six. The weather is supposed to stay clear, and not too hot, so I thought an outdoor buffet would be nice. If I extend the patio table, and carry over the two picnic tables, we can seat almost thirty guests."

"Really? I thought you said just a *few* people were coming?"

"I know, but word spread quickly," said Dad, "and before I knew it, everybody was talking about it."

I pushed my food around my plate, still not hungry. I hoped this stomach bug would be gone by Saturday. "What are we celebrating exactly, other than your PhD?"

"Technically, I don't even have it yet, but yes, finishing that endless paper and a couple other announcements."

"Like what?"

"You'll see."

His silly grin was starting to bother me.

"Come on, Dad, give me a hint."

"Well, it's not official yet," he said, "but one announcement may have to do with the funding of the new performance hall."

I almost dropped my glass of milk. "Please don't say it was the Lockharts."

"Nope, not the Lockharts."

"Phew." I couldn't imagine having to interact with Lux at more horrible dinner parties.

"They lost interest as soon as they found out they couldn't erect a statue of themselves in front of the building."

We both burst out laughing at the same time.

"I actually feel kind of sorry for Lux, with those two for parents."

"You've had quite the change of heart," said Dad. "I seem to remember you saying she'd ruined your entire life."

"She did. But now that I don't have to see her in school anymore, I'm happy to forget all about her."

"Good," said Dad. "And even if you did go back to live in Kettleboro, she wouldn't be there."

"What do you mean?"

"They're moving again. This time to Texas. Something about an oil field."

"Wait. Did you say *if you go back to live in Kettleboro?*"

"Well, it all depends on Mo. Right now, she has primary custody of you, Agnes."

That didn't worry me at all. As long as Dad didn't change his mind, I knew Mo wouldn't be the problem. She had her new family to replace me.

Chapter 24

A scraping noise woke me up Saturday morning. It sounded like the patio door downstairs sliding open and closed, over and over again. The sunlight shining through the curtains was faint, so I knew it was very early. I rolled onto my side and buried my head under my pillow to block the noise. But it didn't work.

"Morning!" Dad chirped as I dragged my feet down the stairs still in my pajamas.

He was carrying a stack of wooden bowls. And humming. It had been a long time since I'd heard him hum.

"What are you doing?"

"Getting ready for the party!"

"Already?" I plopped down in a kitchen chair and dropped my head on the table. "It's so early, Dad, and you're making a racket."

Tutu nuzzled under my legs and licked my ankles.

"There's a lot to do," he chirped again.

I had never seen him like this. It's not that he wasn't a cheerful person. But he was always cool about it.

After Dad made two more trips back and forth to the patio, I mumbled, "Want some help?" really hoping he didn't.

"Maybe later," he replied as he opened the cabinet and studied the glasses. "I need to get organized first."

I decided to slip out of the house before he changed his mind.

After getting dressed and grabbing a granola bar, I headed outside. I almost stepped on Tutu, who was sitting on the porch and wagging her tail like she wanted a walk, which surprised me. Ever since that first day when we came across Beryl on the dirt road, I'd only taken Tutu on short walks. We'd never gone past the bridge into Renew again. Partly to keep my two worlds separate. But mostly because it was too far for her to go. Lately, even getting to the bridge seemed to be too much for her, so now we strolled around the meadow together once or twice a day. She hadn't been this enthusiastic in weeks, but

I really wanted to check the farm stand since Fin had said he'd be back by the weekend.

"I promise I'll walk you in about an hour," I told her. "Wait right here for me." She flopped down on the porch floor and closed her eyes as if she understood.

I had never taken my bike out this early and it felt different. So much quieter than usual. Peaceful and calm. I couldn't stop smiling, thinking about how wonderful my life would be living permanently in Bittersweet every day with Dad.

The bridge was slick with morning mist as I pedaled slowly across to the other side. I gently leaned my bike against the corner of the store and peered in the window. It was dark inside, even though I thought they opened at six every morning. I could see a bell with a sign next to the cash register, which meant Stella and Birdie were probably out back in the kitchen making the donuts.

Across the street, the farm stand was still closed up like it had been all week. I wondered where Fin could have gone and if it had anything to do with what he had told me. Every time I thought about his life, and the obstacles he'd had to face, it made my problems seem so small.

Before I knew it, I was pedaling down the road toward Fly Back Farm. It was possible Fin had arrived home already but hadn't had a chance to open up the stand. I decided that as soon as I saw him I would tell him everything.

I parked my bike near the stone posts and scanned the property. The barn door swung open and Harriet appeared, followed by Beryl, who rushed over to a patch of feathery grass.

"Chloe? What are you doing up so early?" She wore high rubber boots and carried a bucket.

"Hi, Harriet. Is Fin back?"

"Not yet. Come help me feed the critters." She handed me a scooper and we took turns tossing seed to the geese and chickens. "I'm driving to the airport later this afternoon to pick him up. Do you want to come with me?"

"All the way to the airport in Burlington?"

"Actually he's landing at the little strip not far up the river. It's for small private planes."

The scoop slipped out of my hand, spilling the seed in a heap. "Fin flies his own plane?"

"Not yet, but I know he would love to someday," she said. "Didn't he tell you where he was going?"

"No."

I picked up the scoop and glanced back at Beryl, who was grazing close behind us. It almost felt as if she was listening.

"It's pretty exciting." Harriet smiled. "I'll let him tell you all about it."

If Fin was flying on a private plane, obviously he had even more secrets about himself.

"I wish I could go with you, but I can't." I handed her the scooper. "I've got something going on at our house later today. But can you tell him I stopped by?"

"Of course."

Just before I reached my bike, Harriet called back to me. "Hang on a minute, Chloe! There's something else."

Her voice changed, as if she'd remembered bad news. I waited until she caught up.

"I know Fin talked with you about his adoption."

I stared down at the ground, not sure what to say. "A little bit."

"I don't know if he mentioned that I was very young, barely a teenager when it happened."

"I figured that, since you don't look like a mom. I mean—"

"I know what you mean," she said. Her face softened. "What he probably didn't tell you was that giving up Fin nearly destroyed me. But my parents were in poor health and, as it turned out, they both passed away not long after Fin was born. So I was alone and taking care of myself before I was eighteen years old. I couldn't have taken care of a baby too."

It was hard to imagine being all alone at such a young age. I nodded, like I understood, but then took a few steps back. I really didn't want to talk about something so complicated.

"Listen," she continued, stepping toward me, "I'm telling you all of this because you seem close to Fin and I can tell he trusts you. And I want you to know, Chloe, that despite some complex personal challenges, Fin's had a very good life with his parents in Montreal. They absolutely adore him and have given him some phenomenal opportunities. I mean, all those years and years of—"

She paused, as if she wasn't sure she should tell me more. But now I was interested in hearing what she had to say.

"Years and years of what?" I asked.

She glanced over at Beryl, then bit her lip. "Has Fin told you about, you know, his day-to-day life in Canada?"

I had no idea what she was talking about. "No, he hasn't said much."

"Well . . . You know what, it doesn't matter. You'll see him soon enough." She seemed to change her mind about something. "Anyway, have a good afternoon with your folks." She started walking backwards, swinging the empty bucket. "I'm sure we'll see you soon, Chloe!"

Hearing her call me Chloe, over and over again, felt awful. I couldn't let another day go by pretending to be someone I wasn't. I was tired of all my lies. The minute I saw Fin, I would set things straight. First with him, and then with everyone else.

xxx

As soon as I coasted into the driveway, I scanned the yard for Tutu. Less than an hour had passed, so I assumed she'd still be sleeping on the porch, but she wasn't there.

Her bed in the back hall was empty and there was no sign of her in the kitchen. I poked my head in the fridge, but nothing looked good. It was strange—I felt icky and hungry at the same time. And had felt that way all week.

Dad slid open the patio door. "Can you hand me some paper towels, Agnes? I need to wipe down the chairs."

I found a new roll under the sink and tossed it across the room. "Where's Tutu?" I asked.

"Haven't seen her. I thought she was with you."

I followed him out back and whistled. "Tutu? Come 'ere, girl!"

"She's probably out in the middle of the meadow sleeping in the hay," said Dad.

All at once I noticed bouquets of flowers and bright tablecloths on every table. Extra chairs were grouped around the edges. Dad had done an amazing job getting everything ready, even stringing lights between the house and two trees.

"Wow, it looks great out here."

He started wiping down the coolers lined up near the grill. "Do you think ten bags of ice are enough?"

I shrugged. "Sounds about right. Are you sure there isn't anything I can do?"

"I'm all set," he said and rubbed his hands together. "The caterer will do the rest."

"A caterer? I thought you were going to buy some pre-made party plates at the grocery store."

"As it turns out we're having an extra special guest, so I need to impress him."

"Someone famous?"

His silly grin was back and he silently nodded.

"Wow. Someone you know personally?"

"I've never met him, but believe me, this will be a night to remember."

A sharp pain cramped across my lower back. "Ugh. I'm not feeling well again, maybe from waking up so early."

Dad set the paper towels on the grill and wrapped his arms around me. "Why don't you go back to sleep, Agnes? I really don't need your help and it might be a late night."

At that moment, nothing sounded better than a nap. "But what about Tutu?"

"I promise I'll take a lap around the meadow and get her in a few minutes. Now go rest up before the party."

I climbed the stairs to my bedroom, kicked off my flip-flops, and pulled the curtains closed. I thought of powering up my phone, but decided I'd check it later during the party. I would need something to do to keep myself from losing my mind with boredom.

Before crawling into bed, I used the bathroom. When I stood up to flush, the water was red. I looked down at my underpants and saw blood. Not spotting, but real blood.

My period.

No wonder I had been feeling so strange. And this had to be the worst possible day to get it.

Or maybe not.

I could tell Dad, and he might let me stay in bed during the party.

Then it occurred to me that I still hadn't bought supplies, hoping I wouldn't need them all summer. So I wadded up some tissues and stuffed them in my shorts for the time being. Then I searched through every cabinet in the bathroom. When nothing turned up, I raced down to the hall bathroom, starting to feel panicky. Nothing there either. Finally, I found a small box of pads in Dad's bathroom, technically Julia's bedroom. For the first time since I'd arrived, I was glad we were staying in a home owned by a woman. I took the box back to my bathroom.

Even though I never did read the book on *becoming a woman*, the school nurse had gone over everything in class one day. So I basically knew what to do, except how to wash my underwear and shorts.

But they were so stained, I ended up shoving them in the trash can.

I caught a glimpse of myself in the mirror and felt sad, as if my childhood was officially over. I had known this day would eventually come, but I'd hoped I could put it off as long as possible.

I crawled into bed and cuddled up under the covers like a little kid.

Snuggled between pillows with my head under the sheets, I thought about Viva and wondered how she'd felt when she got her period. I wished she was around so I could ask her. Mo, of course, would want to be informed right away. Lately she'd stopped bugging me with endless texts and voicemails, just as she'd promised. But knowing she would make an enormously big deal out of this, like she did with everything, was more than I could bear right now.

So I yawned, rolled over, and decided I would call her tomorrow.

Chapter 25

A knock on the door.

I pulled back the covers.

Another knock.

"Agnes? It's time to wake up."

I opened my eyes, then squinted at the late-afternoon sunlight glowing through the edges of the curtains. One of my pillows had fallen on the floor. I leaned over to pick it up and tucked it under my head. The clock on the desk said it was a few minutes past five. Somehow I had slept all day. My stomach ached and I remembered my period. I lifted the covers and was relieved to see the sheets were clean.

More knocks, but louder this time. "Can I come in?" asked Dad.

"No," I groaned. "Not yet."

The silence on the other side of the door felt heavy, like the moment before an alarm goes off. "Our guests will be here soon," he said. "Can you get dressed and come downstairs, please?"

The guests? Oh no, the guests.

I couldn't believe we were having a party when I was feeling like this.

"Can I take something? I'm still not feeling very well."

Dad threw open the door as if I'd called for an ambulance.

"But you've been asleep all day. Are you sick?"

He wore light tan pants and a freshly ironed shirt. His hair was slicked back as if he'd decided to try gel for the first time.

"I'm okay. I just have a headache. I probably slept too long."

He disappeared out the door, then reappeared a minute later with a pill and a glass of water. He sat on the edge of my bed and felt my forehead.

"You don't have a fever, which is good. Take your time, honey, and come down when you're ready. I can handle everyone on my own until you join us."

I didn't have the heart to ask him if I could stay in my room all night. But after a long, hot shower,

I felt a little better. I changed my underwear and pad again. Only ten pads were left in the box, which was probably enough for one more day. I wasn't sure. It didn't say anything in the directions about how often to change them.

Since this party seemed to be a big deal for Dad, I chose something a bit nicer than my usual shorts and flip-flops. Mo had insisted I pack a dress and a pair of wedged sandals that she'd bought before I left for the summer. I figured now was a good time to use them, even though the dress was wrinkled and smelled musty.

In the background I heard voices and laughter, like someone was telling jokes to a large crowd, which made me even more reluctant to go downstairs. But I knew I had to make myself go. This was Dad's big day.

I took a deep breath and opened my bedroom door. Peering over the edge of the railing, I saw a sea of adults, several with bald heads and gray beards. The usual college crowd.

As soon as I reached the bottom of the stairs, one of the grown-ups turned around.

"Agnes!" said Roger, who was holding a plate of appetizers. "You have to try one of these cheesy hors d'oeuvres. They're divine."

"No thanks, I'm not really hungry."

Roger was grinning harder than usual, as if he wanted to say something, but wasn't sure if he should. "Dot is outside waiting for you. Why don't you go outside and find her?"

I glanced around, trying to see if there was anyone else I knew, but saw no one under forty years old.

This was going to be a long night.

The minute I slid open the glass door to look for Dot, a loud, bossy voice drowned out all the others. I knew that voice.

"Agnes! There you are!"

Mo waved both hands over her head from the other side of the patio, like she was flagging down help on the side of the road.

I couldn't move. As it turned out, I didn't have to. Mo bulldozed her way straight through the crowd and, before I knew it, my head was crushed against the side of her neck.

"Holy moly, you've grown, Agnes Moon! And you're wearing that dynamite dress I picked up at the church flea market. I told you it would come in handy."

"What are you doing here, Mo?"

"Oh, one thing led to another. Little Georgie got homesick for his mother, plus our renter in Kettleboro moved out—something about mold in the kitchen cabinets—so we came back a few weeks early."

"No, I mean *here* here. What are you doing in Bittersweet?"

She didn't answer. Instead she turned and waved her arms over her head again. "Richard! Georgie! Come see Agnes!"

"Oh please," I moaned to myself, "tell me this isn't happening."

Mo whipped around again and gripped both of my shoulders. "It looks like they're in the buffet line already. We'll see them soon enough. But tell me," she said, now shaking my shoulders, "how the heck are you? Nice digs you and your dad have here for the summer. And, by the way, Timothy is looking swell." She suddenly lowered her voice. "Any updates you can give me on the status of his health?"

I could only stare at her, still not completely convinced she was real.

"Agnes, you're up!"

Out of nowhere, my dad appeared. The last time I'd seen my parents standing this close to each other, Dad had rented a U-Haul and was moving out.

"Surprise!" he said, pointing at Mo. "I told you we were having a few special guests. The whole gang's here."

I searched the crowd. "Even Viva?"

My parents glanced at each other, then at me.

"We couldn't get a hold of your sister," said Mo, "but we brought Megan!"

"You did . . . *what?*"

That's when I spotted Dot sitting at one of the picnic tables. She was across from another girl whose long, highlighted hair I easily recognized.

Dot and Megan? Together?

My head began to throb. The medicine Dad gave me wasn't working at all.

Mo grabbed my hand. "Yoo-hoo, Megan?" she called as she dragged me across the patio. "Your long-lost BFF has been found again!"

Megan turned around slowly, then climbed over the bench. It felt like I hadn't seen her in years. We stared at each other without speaking.

"Whatever's going on between you two," Mo yelled, "hug it out, girls!"

Like always, I glared at my mother, not that this had ever stopped her before.

"Hi," I finally muttered to Megan.

Megan grinned. "Hi." Then looked down at her feet. "I hope it's okay that I came?"

I knew Megan needed me to say something, but I was at a complete loss for words. I couldn't figure out why Dad had invited any of them. I didn't want them to be here. This was all wrong. I honestly would have preferred spending the whole evening with Dot.

"Sit down and I'll get you girls some fixings," Mo insisted, pushing me toward the table. "We already met your little pal, Deb, over there. Can I get you anything to eat, Deb?"

"Dot," said Dot. "And no thank you. My father is already in the buffet line."

Then she raised her fingers at me in a tiny wave, but she didn't smile.

"Sorry, this is kind of weird and confusing," I told Megan. "I thought my mother was still in Kansas."

She nodded as if she found it weird and confusing too. "I think they got back a couple days ago. Your mom called my mom to invite me up here. Maybe I shouldn't have come."

This was all too much to absorb.

"Do you two live next door to each other?" asked Dot.

I had already forgotten she was there, listening to us. "No, not next door."

"In the same neighborhood?" Dot persisted.

"Nope."

"Can you walk to each other's houses?"

I glared a little. "What does it matter?"

"It's just that you never replied to any of my texts," Megan suddenly blurted, sounding hurt. "I wanted to call you and explain everything about Lux. She was so horrible after you left. I haven't seen her all summer."

"You haven't?"

"Lux!" said Dot. "That's where I've heard your name. Lux mentioned you a couple of times at my house."

Now I felt sick all over again.

Megan stared at Dot. "How do *you* know Lux?"

At that moment, my dad rang a bell, saving me from explaining the whole Lux ordeal on top of everything else. "Thank you for coming, everyone," he said loudly. "I've got some announcements to make, so please help yourselves to the refreshments and then take a seat."

Mo dropped two plates heaped with food in front of Megan and me. Then she climbed awkwardly over the bench and plopped down on my right side. George and Richard appeared behind her holding their own plates.

"G'day Miss Agnes!" said the butler. "'Tis a fine evening for a shindig." At least he wasn't wearing the dumb jacket.

I rolled my eyes. "How do you even know those words, George?"

Richard bent his head and mumbled something. I had no idea what it was, so I turned back to my plate. The sour smell of barbeque chicken wings made me nauseous.

Roger sat across from us, next to Dot, and slipped a dish in front of her. She picked up her fork and pushed a piece of macaroni around her plate.

"I see you found everyone, Agnes!" said Roger, beaming at Mo and Megan. "Were you surprised?"

It occurred to me that Roger was constantly cheerful, like a wind-up toy. The exact opposite of Dot.

"You should have seen her face," yelled Mo. "As if we were aliens beamed down from a flying saucer."

My arm brushed Megan's as I picked up my napkin. She smiled cautiously at me and looked away.

Despite everything, I was starting to feel a tiny bit glad to see her.

"Can we all please raise our glasses?" Dad called out to the crowd.

Everyone lifted a glass at the same time. So I picked up my cup of water and held it near my chest, hoping this would all be over very quickly, and I could go back to bed.

"I can't tell you how much I appreciate having you here tonight. Every single one of you. As most of you know, my dissertation has been *years* in the making."

A bunch of people laughed, then Mo jabbed her elbow in my side and winked. I didn't think it was funny, since it seemed to be one of the main reasons my parents got divorced.

"So I'm thrilled to announce," he continued, "that it is finally complete and approved. And I'm already scheduled to defend it at the end of September."

The crowd cried, "Cheers!" and clinked their glasses.

Mo clinked mine so hard, water splashed on my arm.

"Thank you," said Dad, "but that's only one of the milestones I'm celebrating tonight. It's no secret that we at Prelude Conservatory have been dreaming for years of building a state-of-the-art performance hall. And because of the generosity of our very special guest tonight, that dream is finally coming true."

"Hear, hear!" yelled Roger and a few others, as if we were in some old-fashioned movie.

I had forgotten an extra special guest was coming to this thing. Whoever it was, he couldn't be more of a shock than seeing Mo and her entourage from Kettleboro.

"Without further ado," said Dad, "please give a big round of applause for—not only a very magnanimous benefactor—but the most gifted young cellist in the world today. Who, I might add, has just flown in from his lawyer's office to sign the papers."

It always came back to the cello. I sighed and looked down at my plate.

"Ladies and gentlemen, I present to you the one and only, Finley von Zimmermann!"

Roger almost knocked over the table as he jumped to his feet and pounded his hands together. "Bravo! BRAVO!!"

I stood up like everyone else and turned to watch as the glass door slid open. Someone stepped out onto the patio to thunderous applause. It was hard to see him beyond the wall of bodies, but then the crowd sat down and there he was standing next to my father. A pale boy with messy red hair.

Fin?

Mo jabbed my side again. "Can you believe a kid like him has that much dough?"

I whipped around to face Dot, praying Fin wouldn't notice me. My mind began to race as I wondered how I hadn't known this about him, and what I would say or do if he saw me.

"Finley, our fine fellow!" I heard Dad exclaim. "Would you like to say a few words to your admirers?"

I didn't dare turn around to look. But Fin must have said no, because everyone chuckled and then Dad began talking again.

"He's a very modest young man, but you should all know that Finley here won the Wiesinger International Young Musician Award last year in Vienna when he was fourteen years old. Then he took a little break from performing for personal reasons, and now we're ecstatic to have him back and living in our neck of the woods. I just found out he has a relative over in Renew."

This couldn't be happening. It didn't make sense.

Fin had never even mentioned anything about playing an instrument.

As Dad listed Fin's accomplishments, I thought back to all our conversations, trying to recall if he'd given me any hints about being a world-famous musician. Obviously, he'd been hiding this information about himself, but I couldn't imagine why this would be harder to talk about than what he'd already told me. And why, of all instruments, did he have to play the cello?

When I glanced up, I saw Dot staring at me. She raised her eyebrows as if to ask what was wrong. I picked up my fork and forced myself to take a bite of potato salad. It took everything to make myself swallow. Then I stared down at my plate . . . I'd had this exact potato salad somewhere else.

"And speaking of Renew, before I forget," said Dad, "I want to ask our hard-working caterer to come out of the kitchen and join us. Can someone get the young lady from Birdie's?"

My mouth clamped shut and I couldn't open it. Then my head swiveled just enough to see the glass doors slide open again.

"Here she comes," Dad called, followed by more clapping as another person walked out onto the patio.

Stella. How could this be happening?

She hurried over and stood on the other side of Fin. I could tell they were surprised to see each other by the way they both smiled.

"In case any of you are interested, Birdie's caters all sorts of occasions," said Dad. "We'll certainly be calling on you, Stella, for events up at the Conservatory!"

"Thank you, Professor Moon," she said cheerfully, then pushed her glasses higher on her nose. "I'm so glad you're all enjoying the buffet."

I realized I had twisted all the way around in my seat, because suddenly I saw Fin studying me. His expression shifted from confusion to a wide grin, then back to confusion. I twisted around and noticed Dot still watching me too. My heart was fluttering so hard I thought it might explode. In a moment of panic, I considered slipping under the picnic table and crawling behind the house. But I forced myself to keep calm with my back to the crowd. As soon as this horror show was over, and Dad stopped talking, I would dash around to the front porch and run upstairs.

Megan leaned into me. "This party seems like a really big deal for your father."

I could only nod. It was hard to believe that a few minutes ago I was worried about talking to Megan. Right now, Megan was the least of my problems.

Just when it didn't seem possible for things to get worse, a lady's voice shouted, "You have one more announcement to make, Timothy Moon!"

This time the sliding door crashed open with a bang. I managed to peek over and see the back of a blond woman in a sleeveless black dress.

"Who the heck is that?" Mo blurted to no one in particular.

"Julia?" said Dad. "I can't believe you made it!"

Julia?

She ran across the patio on her high-heeled toes and kissed my dad on the mouth right in front of everyone.

"Good grief," said Mo, jabbing me for the tenth time, "what a drama queen."

The guests stood and raised their glasses again. I stayed in my seat, half of me still hiding while the other half crumbled.

"This is quite a surprise," said Dad. "Friends and colleagues, our esteemed conductor of the Prelude Conservatory Orchestra and owner of this fine house, Dr. Julia Blunt, appears to be back from Argentina a whole month early!"

"Excuse me, professor, but you forgot the fiancée part?" she added and smooched him again.

The what part?

"I guess it's no longer a secret!" said Dad, laughing nervously. "Yes, my fiancée, Dr. Julia Blunt."

Roger sprang to his feet and pounded his hands together. "Congratulations! Hear, hear! *Bravissimo!*"

"Did you know about this?" Megan and Mo asked me at the exact same time.

The voices of the crowd began to blend together and the trees rippled, like they were melting. I held onto the edge of the table as if the Earth was tipping over.

"I have to say, it's been a memorable summer," said Dad, who couldn't seem to stop talking and talking. "However, now it's time to eat, drink, and be merry. But before we do, I want to pay a special tribute to my lovely daughter, Agnes. She's been so patient these last couple of months, hanging around a strange place all by herself, while I barricaded myself upstairs in the office. It's hard to believe she's already twelve years old and growing up so fast. Come join me up here, sweetheart. Everyone wants to see you!"

My head shook *no* over and over as I slumped under the table, trying to disappear.

"AG-*nes*, AG-*nes*," the mob began to chant.

I stared at Dot, as if she could somehow get me out of this, as if she could speak for me—telling them no to being Agnes, no to being twelve years old, no to being anyone's future stepdaughter. No to being at this nightmare of a party.

Mo and Megan were on their feet, clapping and calling my name along with everyone else. But Dot stayed seated and stared right back at me, like I was an injured animal caught in a trap, and she wasn't sure how to help.

"Don't be shy, Agnes!" hollered Mo, who was physically lifting me by my right elbow. "Go on up."

As I stumbled forward and moved through the crowd, I folded my head to my chest, hoping to appear less recognizable.

But I heard them anyway. Two voices: a girl's voice and a boy's voice rising above all the other voices.

"Chloe?"

The slow, swishy words changed over to muffled underwater sounds. And then my whole body felt cold.

Someone grabbed me. It was Julia. She was saying something in my ear.

"Agnes, honey, do you know where my little Tutu went? I searched all over the house when I got here a few minutes ago and I can't find her anywhere."

The people and the patio twirled faster and faster, like one of those spinning amusement park rides that keep you screaming *sssttooopppppp*, but speed up more and more until you feel like you're going to pass out.

Chapter 26

The lamp next to my bed clicked on and I opened my eyes. Dad leaned over my right side while Mo hovered above my left. All I could see were their two faces. For a second, I forgot they were divorced and belonged to other people now.

"Where's Tutu?" I asked.

"Agnes is awake!" said Mo. "She can talk!"

Dad shushed her and they both stood up. Now I could see another person, an older woman with white hair and brown eyes.

"I'm a friend of your father's, Agnes," she said calmly. "Do you mind if I listen to your heart?"

A stethoscope hung from her neck and she was carrying a black bag.

Obediently, I took deep breaths as she listened. After slipping a thermometer in my mouth, and taking my blood pressure, she poked at my neck and stretched my eyelids.

"All her vitals seem fine," she told my parents. Then she gazed down at me with a puzzled look. "Anything bothering you, Agnes?"

"I've lost Tutu" was all I could say.

"Everyone is out in the field looking for her," Dad said. "Don't worry, honey. We'll find her."

I didn't believe him. I didn't know if I could believe anyone ever again. "You were supposed to get her. You *promised* you would get her."

"Is there anything else going on?" the woman asked.

I closed my eyes and clenched my teeth. Even if I were to answer that question, where would I start?

"Ah–ha!" Mo yelled from the bathroom.

She emerged holding the small box of pads.

"You got your period, Agnes! I knew it. You're a woman now!"

Normally, nothing could have humiliated me more than that ridiculous statement. But nothing felt normal anymore, and all the humiliation I had stored up inside of me had been used up at the party.

"When did you get your first period?" the doctor

asked gently, as if to say she understood my mother was part of the problem.

"Today," I mumbled.

Out of the corner of my eye, I saw Dad back up and slump against the wall. I wanted him to leave. I wanted all of them to leave.

"Well, that explains it," said Mo, smacking her hands on her thighs.

"Not exactly," said the doctor. "It's common to feel lightheaded or possibly faint with menarche, but it's quite unusual to pass out cold."

"Should we take her to the hospital?" asked Dad.

"No!" I shouted and threw back my covers. "You should all leave me alone and stop ruining my life and just find Tutu! *Please* find Tutu."

I rolled over, pulled the sheet over my head, and sobbed into my pillow.

I heard Mo say, "Now what do we do?"

"Let her sleep if she can and go find the dog," said the doctor. "I'll be down at the party. We can chat before I leave."

The harder I cried, the more my stomach cramped which made me cry even more. Just when I'd thought my life was finally getting better—a fresh start in a new place, alone with my dad—it instantly became a hundred times worse than it had ever been. If I let myself really think about what had happened, what I had done, and the shame of it all, I knew I would never stop sobbing. Every catastrophe seemed worse than the next, impossible to fix.

At some point, through my tears, I became aware that my parents were sitting on either side of my bed, by my feet. I couldn't understand why they seemed more concerned about me than Tutu.

"Why won't you leave me alone? I know you don't care about me anymore."

Mo rubbed my leg while Dad squeezed my ankle. I wanted to pull away, but I couldn't. Because I knew it would be the last time they would hold on to me together, before they would let go forever and hold onto other people.

"Nothing could be further from the truth," said Mo. "However, your dad and I are starting to see how tough this past year has been on you."

"And we're so sorry about that," added Dad. "We want to make things better."

I sniffed back my tears and wiped my arm across my wet face. "How? You're getting married and Mo has a whole new family. I have no one."

"What are you talking about?" said Mo. "You have a posse of people who love you and want the best for you, especially your dad and me. We will always be your parents first, Agnes, before anyone or anything else in our lives."

"Always," said Dad.

I wanted to believe them, but I still had so many doubts.

"Listen, I know meeting Julia this way must have come as a shock," Dad said, followed by a long pause. "I tried to tell you about her, so many times, but it was clear you weren't ready. Then she surprised me by flying in a whole month early. Julia had no idea that you didn't know about the engagement, honey. That's my fault. I'm so sorry for not being upfront. With both of you," he said as he looked at Mo.

Keeping the whole truth about Julia from me wasn't nearly as dishonest as what I'd done, but still it was painful to hear my dad's apology. It made me wonder if Fin could accept mine, or even speak to me ever again.

Suddenly, the door flew open and banged against the wall.

"WE FOUND HER!" yelled Julia.

She was barefoot, but still in her fancy black dress, which was now covered in dirt. In her arms was Tutu.

"Hallelujah!" Mo yelled even louder.

Dad sighed with relief. "Where was she?"

I wiped the rest of my tears away so I could see her clearly. Julia placed Tutu on my lap. She was shaking, so I pulled her close and kissed her soft head.

"When we didn't find her in the meadow," said Julia, still out of breath, "most of us headed to the woods. But then von Zimmermann, all on his own, discovered her sitting at the corner of the little stone bridge that crosses over to Renew. Like she was waiting for someone."

Me. Tutu was waiting for me.

"Fin found her?" I asked.

"Fin?" said Dad. "You mean Finley?"

I nodded, then turned away. Now was not the time to explain that part of my life.

"Honestly," said Julia, "that young man saved the day. It was as if he knew exactly where Tutu would be."

Part of me was glad to know Fin was the one who'd found Tutu, but a bigger part didn't want to think about him at all, because that would remind me of the mess I'd made of everything.

"You were supposed to wait for me on the front porch," I whispered into her furry ear, "not wander off searching for me."

The three adults huddled over my bed.

"It's wonderful seeing you look happier, Agnes," said Dad. To Mo and Julia, he added, "Let's give these two space to rest. We still have some guests to tend to downstairs."

"Good idea," said Mo. "You and your conductor gal can skedaddle, and I'll stay here with Agnes."

As the two of them headed toward the door, I was surprised to hear myself say, "Thank you, Julia."

She paused and turned around.

"For what, Agnes?"

"For not being mad about Tutu. And for letting me take care of her this summer."

She grinned, displaying her mouthful of sparkling white teeth. "The summer isn't over yet!"

I wasn't so sure about that.

As soon as the door closed, Mo said, "So I have to ask you. Was your father ever actually sick?"

So much for giving me space to rest. I groaned and buried my face in my pillow. "No. I'm sorry, Mo. I made it up. I wanted so badly to come here this summer and . . ."

"And your wicked old mom was going to drag you away."

I peered out from the folds of the pillowcase. "I wouldn't call you wicked."

"But you wanted to get away from me so much that you . . ." She trailed off.

"Lied." I finished it for her. "I lied. I lied to a lot of people this summer, Mo. It wasn't just you."

"Yes, we pieced that together when someone called you Chloe."

Another moan escaped me. "I know I messed up. But can we talk about it later? Please? I'm so tired."

Mo opened her mouth as if she was about to say something else, but then—miraculously—she closed it. After another second or two she said, "Okay. There's one more thing, though. Would you really rather live with your dad than with me?"

Dad must have already talked over the custody agreement with her. Maybe that's why he wanted to bring the whole family together today.

For the first time in my life, I felt a little sorry for my mother. "I thought so," I replied, "but . . ."

"But what?"

I could tell she wanted to hear that I would miss her too much or that I didn't want to leave my life in Kettleboro. But none of that was true. And yet, living with Dad wasn't going to be what I'd expected either. All the things I'd resented Mo for—moving on, getting a new family, changing our lives—were things that Dad had done too, without even telling me.

I remembered Fin's answer when I asked about his connection to Harriet, so I said, "It's complicated, Mo."

She nodded slowly. For once she didn't seem to have anything to say.

I forced myself to smile. "And I really am tired. I just want to sleep."

She patted my back. Something about the way she did it felt sad yet soothing at the same time. "Got it."

xxx

A minute after she left, there was another knock at the door.

"Mo, I really—"

"It's me." Dot walked in, holding a plate of food. She carefully placed it on the night table. "You didn't eat much at dinner. Are you feeling any better?"

The barbequed chicken didn't smell so bad anymore.

"I am," I said, and I meant it. "Are you and your dad leaving?"

"In a few minutes. Roger hasn't talked to every single person yet."

I couldn't help grinning.

"What about you?" she asked.

"What about me?"

"Are you going back to Kettleboro?"

I sighed, thinking of how confidently Julia had swept out onto the patio—*her* patio at *her* house. Tutu was *her* dog. Dad was *her* fiancé. Nothing about this place belonged to me. "I guess I should."

"That's too bad," said Dot. "You're the best friend I've ever had, Agnes."

I sat up and pulled Tutu closer. The fact that Dot thought I had been a friend at all made me realize how lonely she must be, and how terrible I had been to her.

"We can text each other," I said.

"Really?" She moved a little closer and pulled her smartphone out of the pocket of her pleated skirt. "Can I have your number?"

I took her phone, added my info, and handed it

back to her. She stared at it so long, I wondered if she had any other contacts.

"I'd better go," she finally said. "Tutu is making my nose itch. Will you let me know when you come back to visit your dad?"

As it turned out, I was glad I had confided in Dot. In a way, she was the one person in the world who got me.

"You bet, Vladlena."

Chapter 27

When I woke up the next morning, Tutu was curled up against my back. I climbed out of bed slowly, so I wouldn't wake her.

On the bureau was a small box of pads—no bow this time—with a note: *Picked these up at your local Fred's Meds last night. Come home soon, Agnes. We miss you. Love, Mo & the gang.*

At the very bottom of the paper was another note: *I miss you too. Megan.*

Somehow, in all the chaos, I had forgotten about Megan.

The fact that she came all the way from Kettle-boro with my ridiculous family, knowing how upset I was with her, made me believe we could be friends again. Maybe even best friends.

My stomach growled. I'd never eaten the food

Dot left on my night table, which someone had taken away. Now I dreaded the thought of going downstairs for breakfast and facing the world, but knew I couldn't stay in this bedroom for the rest of my life.

When I was little, and something seemed too difficult or too scary, Dad always told me to take it one step at a time by putting one foot in front of the other. I never understood how that could help until now.

As soon as I opened the door, Tutu woke up and wagged her tail. The first step would be carrying her downstairs and feeding her.

"Good morning, ladies!"

Julia was sitting alone at the kitchen table reading the newspaper. She wore a plain T-shirt and sweatpants with her hair in a ponytail. A definite improvement from her fancy black cocktail dress, in my opinion.

"Morning," I said calmly, cautiously. Baby steps.

"Gorgeous day," she beamed, then flipped through the pages noisily.

Something about her reminded me of Mo, even though they looked nothing alike. It was that living-out-loud way of filling up the room that they both shared. Bulldozers. You'd think Dad would have gone for the opposite type this time around.

I opened the fridge to get Tutu's canned food, but then remembered all over again that this was Julia's kitchen. And her dog. Not mine.

"Is it okay if, you know, I feed Tutu?"

Julia put down the paper and her mug of coffee, then walked over and leaned against the kitchen island. "Can I tell you something, Agnes?"

The last thing I wanted to hear was a lecture from the woman who was marrying my father, but I didn't want to be rude either. After all, it was her house.

"Sure."

"When I was hired last year and met your dad, do you know the first thing he told me about himself?"

I knew the answer to that one. "That he plays the cello."

"Nope. That he has two incredible daughters he missed every second of the day. His heart was heavy and he was very lonely."

I hadn't expected to hear that. Part of me wondered if she was making it up. But maybe that was because I'd been lying to everybody, including myself, all summer. "Then he shouldn't have left us."

To my surprise, she nodded, as if she agreed. "Adults make lots of mistakes, and sometimes do things that are hurtful, because we have a lot of responsibilities and worries and complications to juggle. That's not an excuse. It's just the way things are."

I looked away, even though she had my attention.

"But do you know the thing we all want most, Agnes?"

"I don't know, more money?"

"Well, that helps," she said and flashed her perfect teeth. "But what we really want more than anything else is the best for the children in our lives. Especially when circumstances are beyond our control."

I wasn't sure what all this had to do with me asking her if I could feed the dog, but I kind of knew what she was trying to say.

"Because I care about your dad, and because I know he will always care about you and your sister more than anyone else on this planet, I want both of you to know this home is your home. That bedroom upstairs is your bedroom. All the food in this kitchen is your food. And little Tutu is your little Tutu too. So you don't have to ask me permission to use anything. Got it?"

That was one of the nicest things anyone had ever said to me. And I kind of liked the way she reminded me of Mo.

"Got it," I said.

Outside, we heard a car pull into the driveway.

"That can't be your dad already," said Julia as she peered out the window over the sink. "He's tied up in a meeting on campus all morning."

I fed Tutu while Julia checked outside. The next thing I knew, I heard voices in the back hall.

"Do you remember the caterer from the party last night, Agnes? She's come by to pick up her supplies. What did you say your name was, young lady?"

I froze. Then Stella froze.

She was holding a stack of plastic crates.

I didn't know what to say or do.

"I'll come back another time," she said and turned away.

"Don't be silly," insisted Julia. "Everything's washed." She rushed over to open the dishwasher. "Do you want help loading? I'm happy to do it."

"Why don't I help?" I heard myself say. Then I looked directly at Julia. "I think Tutu wants to go outside, but someone should probably stay with her."

Unlike Mo, Julia got the hint right away. "Good idea. I'll walk her and let you girls handle this."

Stella set her crates on the floor and began loading the clean plates into them. "It looks like you're feeling better," she said.

I wondered if the entire party had seen me collapse and get carried up the stairs. More humiliating moments I didn't want to think about.

I paused before saying the only thing I could think of to say. "I'm sorry."

Stella didn't look at me as she continued stacking the dishes. "For what?"

I hadn't thought any of this through yet, and had no idea how to explain myself. But then it occurred to me I didn't have to come up with a clever excuse or story anymore. I just needed to tell her the truth.

"I'm sorry for lying to you."

She dropped a handful of silverware between the plates and finally looked at me. The hurt in her eyes made me feel even worse. "Why did you do that, Chloe? I mean, whatever your name is."

"Agnes is my name, and I did it because I thought I hated my name. The same way I hated my hair and my freckles and the way I looked in a bathing suit.

The same way I hated my life. When I crossed the bridge into Renew, I pretended to be someone who had the life I wanted."

She crossed to the other side of the room and sank onto the couch. I waited a minute before sitting next to her.

"I guess I know how all that feels," she said and sighed. "For Pete's sake, I lied to you about Wyatt. But that was the only thing I lied about, and part of it was to protect him. You lied about *everything*. Even your pet rabbit, who's a dog. I mean, are you really only twelve years old?"

My whole face frowned. "Yep." Telling the truth was painful, and so much harder than lying. But at the same time, it was a huge relief.

"I think hearing that shocked me the most," said Stella. "You seem so mature and, I don't know, worldly."

"Maybe it was because you wanted me to be those things?"

"Maybe." Stella sighed again. "So you don't have a cool older sister named Viva?"

"Actually, that's the only part that is true. Except she isn't sick. She's just sick of us and wants nothing to do with our parents. Or me."

"How come?"

"I'm not sure." I could feel my bottom lip start to quiver. I really couldn't let myself cry again, because I knew how hard it would be to stop. "It happened after the divorce. Another thing I lied about. My mother and father aren't married."

"I figured that part out after meeting your dad's fiancée."

The way she said it made me smile a tiny bit. I wondered if someday, far in the future, this would all seem funny.

Stella checked her phone and stood up. "I have to get back to the store. Birdie is watching Wyatt and lately he's getting to be too much for her to handle. One of these days, that boy is going to climb up on the roof and try to fly."

I followed her back to the dishwasher to finish loading her crates.

"I'm so sorry," I said again.

Stella slid her glasses back into place and patted me on the shoulder. "I know you are. So from now on, let's be completely honest with each other. Swear on your great-grandmother's grave, no more lies?"

I nodded. "I swear, no more lies."

Together we carried the crates out to her pickup truck. On the far side of the meadow I could see Julia and Tutu walking near the river.

Stella saw me watching them and said, "She seems really nice."

"I think she probably is."

Stella opened the truck door, but hesitated before climbing in. "This feels like the end of something," she said, "like you're leaving?"

The moment she said that, I knew I had to go back to Kettleboro today and sort things out. "I'll visit soon. Please tell Birdie and Dave how sorry I am."

She nodded. "Can I ask you one last question, Chloe—I mean—Agnes?"

It felt odd hearing her call me Agnes, but it also felt right. "Of course."

"Do you still hate your life? Because I can't imagine why you would. I mean, look at you, girl. You've got *everything* going for you."

I glanced up at the sky and saw a beautiful bird with wide wings and a fanned tail soar overhead. I wondered if it was the same falcon Fin and I had seen at the top of the hill . . . still unsure about where to go.

"I don't think I've ever really hated my life. It's more about not knowing where I belong."

"Well, I hope you figure it out," said Stella. "And don't forget, our door is always open with an extra place at the table. Birdie wouldn't have it any other way."

Then she gave me a hug, which was far more than I ever could have hoped for that day.

Chapter 28

I spent the next couple of hours collecting my stuff and packing my duffel bag. This time I included the box from Mo. For so long, I'd dreaded the day I would get my period. But since getting it, in the middle of everything else that had happened, I'd barely thought about it.

Dad arrived home around lunchtime. I heard him climb the stairs to my bedroom. For a second I thought about hiding my duffel bag, but it seemed too late for that.

"Sorry for being away all morning," he said as he peered around the door, "but there was an important—" He stopped and stared at my bag. "Are you packing, Agnes?"

I nodded, afraid to look up and see the sadness I could hear in his voice.

He took a few steps toward me. "How come?"

"I'm not sure," I said. "I just feel like I need to go back home. Today. The last bus leaves at five. Do you mind giving me a ride to the station?"

"Of course I mind," said Dad. "I refuse to end the summer this way. At least stay a couple more days and get to know Julia. I think you'll like her."

I already knew I liked her. But that had nothing to do with what I was trying to tell him. "You don't understand."

I slid down to the floor and leaned against my bed. Dad folded his legs and sat next to me.

"I really want you to live with me, Agnes," Dad said quietly. "Having Julia with us doesn't change that."

"Actually, it changes everything."

He wrapped his arm around my shoulder. "Tell me what I don't understand, Agnes. Please."

I chose my words carefully. "I had this idea of what living with you would be like. Not exactly the way things were before the divorce, but close enough. If I had known you were going to marry Julia, I wouldn't have gotten my hopes up."

He blinked a few times. Then he rubbed the back of his neck and took a deep breath. "Agnes, you can't think about your life as separate parts. Instead, try to think of it as a tall layer cake. Our family is the foundation, the strong bottom layer, on which your whole life will be built. Just like your mother and I told you, that will never change. But other people will come into our lives, and your life, and they'll add their own special ingredients to more and more layers, making the cake that much richer."

I thought about it for a second and it kind of made sense, even if it didn't make me feel better.

"At least you didn't use a music metaphor," I said and sighed.

Dad grinned and pulled me in for a hug. "So you'll stay?"

My whole body ached with confusion.

"I want to stay, Dad, I really do. But I need to go back to Kettleboro and fix my life there first."

He kissed my forehead. "Okay, I'll drive you to the bus station. But only if you agree to spend more time here than our old once-a-month weekend visits."

"Sure, and I'll even throw in Thanksgiving this year."

We both laughed. It felt like everything was sort of back to normal.

"So when will the new performance hall be built?" I asked, ready to change the subject.

"Within a couple years, I hope."

"That long?"

"That's faster than usual, actually. And our young cellist, Finley, has given us full authority to design and construct it according to our wishes, which is incredibly generous."

I stared down at my lap thinking about the Fin I knew, who was also generous, but in a different way. "Is he going to teach or perform at the college?"

"He might pop in once a year or so, but he's moving back to Montreal soon."

"He is?" I said too quickly. "Why?"

"That's where he lives. Apparently he was staying here temporarily while he was recuperating. We've been working with his manager for years, trying to get him to visit the Conservatory. So it was quite extraordinary that Roger not only discovered Finley living just over the bridge in Renew, but that he was also interested in funding the performance hall."

Fin had never said anything about recuperating. "Do you mean he was staying in Renew because he was sick?"

Dad's face dropped, like he didn't know how to

tell me. "I'm not exactly sure what happened, Agnes, but I'm thrilled to see he's on the mend. We all are."

I nodded, wondering if I would ever know what happened to Fin.

"Well, I guess I'd better let you finish packing," said Dad, getting to his feet. "I'll pop downstairs and make us some lunch."

As he headed for the door, I thought of something else. "Hey Dad?" I asked. "How did Roger find out Finley was living around here?"

He turned back and shrugged. "Apparently, Dot told him."

That didn't make any sense. How would Dot know? I knew I had never mentioned a boy I'd met in Renew. She couldn't possibly have found out about Fin from me.

As soon as Dad closed the door, I grabbed my phone.

Hey, I texted. *How do you know that famous cellist? Finley?*

A few minutes later she replied. *From that night we visited your house for dinner.*

Huh?

When I went out to the car to get my allergy spray, he was standing in the driveway by the barn and I recognized him. I asked if he was looking for your dad, but he said he lived across the bridge and was looking for a girl who lived on this side of the river. Then he left.

Dot! Why didn't you tell me?

Why would I? You think music is boring, especially the cello.

Because I was that girl.

×××

In some ways, I wanted the weather to be drizzly and gray to match my mood. Instead, ribbons of white clouds danced across the blue sky.

After lunch, I automatically headed for the barn to get my bike but changed my mind as soon as I reached the driveway. Despite what Julia had said, it no longer felt like my bike. At least, not yet. So I turned around and walked to Renew, as I had done on that first day.

When I crossed the stone bridge I paused in the middle and stared down at the river. The water was much lower now. The rainbow still arched between the two rocks, but so faintly I could barely see it.

I wanted to slip into the store and apologize to Birdie too. But a sign on the door said they had already closed and would reopen tomorrow. It felt strange thinking that I wouldn't be around tomorrow. Just yesterday morning, before the party, I'd thought I would live here forever.

Across the street, the farm stand looked deserted. The stacked wooden boxes of vegetables were nearly empty. Only a few bouquets of limp flowers were left in the recycled glass jars.

I stared at the dirt road trying to gather the courage to walk down. Finally I took one step forward. And then another, until I was slowly making my way toward the farm. When I arrived at the fork, I thought about veering right and escaping to the covered bridge where Fin and I had first gotten to know each other. That could be my last memory of us, pretending the rest of it had never happened. But I knew I could never live with myself if I didn't turn left.

As I peered at the farm through the stone posts, the first thing I noticed were all the wings. Two ducks were gliding in for a landing, annoying the geese who flapped their feathers at the intruders, as butterflies and flying insects fluttered and buzzed above the rows and rows of flowers.

The screen door up the hill creaked open. I took a deep breath and glanced over, ready to see Fin. But it was Harriet shaking out a tablecloth. All at once I panicked, at a loss for what to say to her. Harriet must know everything by now—unless Fin hadn't told her? I turned to hide, hoping to give myself time to figure out what to do next.

"Hello?"

I turned back.

She stood at the edge of the porch and studied me, almost as if she didn't recognize me. Then she draped the tablecloth over the railing and walked down the hill. Immediately I glued my eyes to the ground, too ashamed to look her in the eye. I could hear her moving closer and closer until she stopped in front of me. My heart raced, but still, I couldn't look up. The next thing I knew, Harriet placed her hand on my shoulder and gently pulled me into her arms.

She knew.

I didn't want to cry, so I didn't hug her back, but a few tears still leaked through and ran down my face.

Chapter 29

After a minute or so, she pulled back. I wiped my eyes and looked up.

Harriet pointed over to the front steps of the porch. "Let's sit down."

As we walked through the damp grass, I glanced around nervously.

"Fin isn't here," she said. "He's up at the college and won't be back for another hour or two."

That meant I wouldn't get the chance to explain everything to him and still make the 5 o'clock bus. I tried to squash my disappointment as we sat down next to each other on the bottom step.

"You know," said Harriet, "when Fin's mother first contacted me last fall, she was very worried about him."

"She was?" I managed to whisper.

"She told me he was sick. Not physically sick so much, more like emotionally sick. She said he was going through a very serious bout of depression. He'd shut down completely."

I didn't know what to say. I knew Fin was dealing with stuff, more than the average person, but I never imagined it was so serious. I tried to imagine the Fin I knew—who was curious and thoughtful and full of life—unable to function.

"How come?" I asked.

She crossed her arms and gazed up at the sky. "There's no easy answer really. Besides, I wouldn't want to speak for him. It's his story to tell when he's ready. But his mother got in touch with me because she needed my help."

I stayed very still, not quite sure why she was telling me this but hoping she would say more.

"Finley," she began again, "was a child prodigy by the time he was seven years old. Do you know what that means?"

"I think so. It means he's gifted, right?"

"Yes, he's a brilliant kid, but he's exceptionally gifted in music. He could identify every note by ear and play any instrument at a very young age. However, he was particularly drawn to the cello."

That familiar jealousy boiled up again. It seemed like everything always came back to the cello.

"By the time he was thirteen, Fin was a world-renowned classical musician. That's a tremendous amount of pressure for any teenager, not to mention a peculiar way to live: touring from continent to continent with your mother, a tutor, and a team of adults. On top of all of that, Fin had additional personal issues he hadn't really ever dealt with fully. One of those issues was me and his adoption."

I shifted in my seat, not sure if I was supposed to say something, but it seemed like Harriet just wanted me to listen.

"So it all came to a head last fall when Fin suddenly stopped. Everything. At once. His mother said his therapist felt it was time Fin and I met each other, so I invited him and his parents here to the farm last December. After only one week, he seemed to be improving, so we all agreed he should stay on his own for a while. And he's been here ever since."

My mind drifted back to the first day we saw each other, through the window at the store. How we'd felt drawn to each other right away. Two kids with secrets.

"Just recently," Harriet continued, "Fin told me that for the first time in his life he feels content. And I know part of feeling that way has to do with you, Agnes. You're the first good friend he's had in a very long time, maybe ever."

I swallowed hard when she said my real name. Now I knew where this was going.

"I'm sorry," I blurted. "I didn't mean for it to happen. It started as a game, but—"

Harriet reached across the table and held my hand. "I know you're sorry. It's written all over your face. And I know how at your age a lot of things can seem like games at first, and then get out of control. But I think for someone like Fin, that's hard to understand. So, what I'm trying to say is, I don't think he can process this right now. Okay?"

It wasn't okay, not really. Even though I had been dreading apologizing to Fin, I knew it was the right thing to do. But maybe Harriet thought seeing me would only make things worse for Fin.

I didn't want to hurt him even more than I already had. "Okay."

"Hey," she said in a more cheerful tone, slapping the wooden step. "I have some good news I think you'll be glad to hear."

I couldn't imagine anything that would sound like good news. "You do?"

"The sign is going back up today."

"Which sign?"

"*Wing Repairs!* I've decided to start rehabbing again."

I couldn't help smiling a little. "That is good news."

"I've decided that one way I can start to fix my own wings is to help others with theirs. Especially now that Fin's ready to fly back home."

I had already heard that news from Dad, but still, it was hard imagining Fin living anywhere but here. "When is he leaving?"

"Next week. He'll be in Montreal for a few months, practicing and preparing, and then take off on another world tour."

I knew this was good news too, because it meant Fin felt well enough to return to his life as a musician. But still, I was upset. As if now there was no hope of regaining our friendship . . . as if the whole summer had never happened.

"I'm actually leaving today."

"What?" Harriet seemed surprised. "You're deserting me too?"

"I'm going back home to live with my mother.

But I'll still visit my dad on weekends and some holidays."

She reached over and squeezed my hand. "Good! Make sure you cross the bridge to Renew whenever you're in Bittersweet. I'll need help with those wing repairs."

I promised I would, even though I knew it would feel a little sad visiting the farm with Fin gone.

Harriet gave me one more hug before I left, and this time I hugged her back. Once we said our good-byes and parted ways, I watched her climb the slope toward the house. I felt a tiny bit better, as if something heavy that had been holding me down was slowly letting me go.

Chapter 30

I took my time walking down the dirt road, wondering if I should write an old-fashioned letter to Fin explaining everything. Not right away, of course, but in a month or so. I could stop by the farm, when I was visiting my dad, and ask Harriet for his address. And maybe by then, she would agree it would be okay for me to contact him and apologize.

About halfway down the road, I noticed a rustling in the woods. At first I didn't see anything. Then a large white nose pushed through a tall bush.

Beryl.

She trotted over to me and buried her head under my arm. "What are you doing out here?" Her skin flickered as I stroked her smooth coat. "I'm so glad to see you, but I think we both know where you need to go . . ."

Just then, a sharp whistle pierced the air. I spun around and saw Fin. He was standing back at the fork under the big tree. I had no idea how he could have gotten there without passing me.

I expected Beryl to immediately trot toward him, but she didn't move from my side. So he whistled again, more sharply. Her tail swooshed at a fly, but she stayed put.

I couldn't decide if I should lead Beryl toward him or if I should wait for him to come over and get her. As it turned out, we both moved forward at the same time.

His hands were in his pockets as he dragged his feet reluctantly across the ground. His head twisted sharply to the side, away from me.

"Hi," I said.

He swiveled his head and stared at something above me. His whole face was filled with such anger and hurt, I barely recognized him.

"Come on, Beryl," he said and turned to leave.

But still, she wouldn't go.

Without thinking about what I should say or what Harriet wanted me to do, I found myself blurting the first thing that came into my head. "You did it to me too, you know, Finley von whatever your snobby last name is. You lied to *me* too!"

He stopped, still facing the other way.

"Beryl, come!" he snapped and continued walking again.

She refused.

"You never told me you were rich and famous and known *all over the world* for playing the cello! *I HATE the stupid cello!*"

He grabbed his head with both hands, then whipped around and glared at me.

"That doesn't even make sense! Why would anyone hate an instrument?"

"Because that instrument destroyed my life. It split up my parents and stole my dad from our family! From me."

As soon as I said it, I realized he was right. It didn't make sense to blame my problems on a chunk of wood and a bunch of strings. Maybe the problem was I had no one to blame.

"I didn't talk about my music," said Fin, "because I wanted to feel *normal*. You have no idea what it's like being famous. It's impossible to have real friendships. I needed *a real friend*."

"So did I."

He inhaled and exhaled a series of exasperated breaths. "Do you have the slightest idea what it took for me to tell you everything I told you?" he finally said. "I trusted you."

"I know. And I'm really sorry. I wish I had been honest with you from the beginning. I just wanted a whole new life where I felt like I belonged. So I experimented and decided to make it a game."

"A game? You lied about every single thing. About your name, your family, your home, and even your age? You're only *twelve* years old."

He said that last part with such disgust, like Stella did, as if being twelve was the worst thing anyone could be.

"You were the one who said age was just a number."

He kicked the ground and made a terrible sound, like he was in pain.

I turned to Beryl for help or some kind of sign, but her head was down, practically touching the ground.

"Fin," I said, gathering all of my courage, "I didn't know I would end up liking you so much. I wanted to tell you the truth, and I was going to, but then that horrible party happened and you found out everything before I had the chance."

He stopped kicking the ground.

"Anyway, I'm going home tonight. And I heard you're leaving too, so we'll probably never see each other again. I just wanted to say that I'm really, really sorry. And also, thank you for finding Tutu."

I turned to leave and to give Beryl one last stroke.

"That part about liking me," said Fin. "Was that before or after I told you?"

I hesitated before turning back and facing him again. "Told me what?"

"About what happened when I was born?"

"Which part?"

Fin's mouth dropped open in disbelief. "The part about being named Abigail?"

"Oh." I paused, trying to figure out the right way to word my answer. "I like you because you're Fin. Knowing what happened when you were born doesn't change that. You're still Fin. Right?"

His whole body softened, and he dropped his arms. "Right."

"To be honest, I'm not sure I would have liked you if I'd known you play the stupid cello."

His eyes were wet, but he laughed a little. Then he wiped his face and sniffed.

"I have an idea," he said.

"What?"

"Meet me at the covered bridge ten years from today."

A gust of wind blew leaves against the back of my legs. "Huh?"

"I mean it. Our ages won't matter then."

Ten years seemed like a lifetime away. I would be twenty-two years old and he would be twenty-five.

Fin pulled out his phone and studied the screen. "In one decade, on August 4th at exactly three o'clock Eastern Standard Time, promise to meet me at the covered bridge, Agnes Moon."

When he said my name I didn't cringe like I always did. "Okay, I promise."

At that moment, Beryl pulled away from me, then strolled past Fin, and continued on toward the farm. As if her work here was done.

Chapter 31

Julia seemed genuinely sad to say goodbye. When she asked if I was leaving because of her surprise visit, I told her I was leaving for a lot of reasons. Which was true. I also told her I was looking forward to seeing her again soon, which was true too.

Dad gave me time to be alone with Tutu out on the porch before loading my stuff into the car. She climbed onto my lap as soon as I sat down on the bottom step. I rubbed her head as I took one last glance around the yard. At the big maple tree, the red barn, and out beyond the meadow to the river.

Leaving Tutu was hardest of all. I kissed the top of her head, between her ears, and told her I would be back soon.

It turned out the bus was running late, so my dad waited with me on a bench outside the station.

"The wind is picking up," he said. "Feels like it might rain later tonight."

I smiled and nodded.

We watched a group of people board a bus to Burlington. Where Viva lived. It seemed like Dad wanted to say something, but instead he sighed and crossed his legs.

Finally, my bus pulled into the driveway and parked a few yards away from us.

"The Kettleboro bus has now arrived at Bay 3," said an announcer. "Kettleboro passengers, please form a line at Bay 3."

I stood up. "I guess that's me."

Dad stayed on the bench and reached for my hand.

"You can still change your mind, Agnes. We can go out to dinner, just the two of us."

I pulled his hand toward me to make him stand.

"Thanks, but I really need to go." I hugged him. "And besides, I think Mo needs me."

"Oh Agnes," Dad whispered, as he pulled me closer. "Both of us will always need you and love you more than you can ever know."

"Last call for the bus to Kettleboro at Bay 3," said the announcer.

"I know," I whispered back.

The minute I exited the bus station back home, someone honked inside the line of waiting cars. A moment later, an arm waved frantically out of the driver's side of a familiar minivan.

I sighed, then laughed a little. Some things would never change.

Richard got out of the passenger seat as I walked over, then he hurried around the car and slipped through the back door.

Mo reached across the seat, as I climbed in front, and squeezed my wrist way too hard.

"Welcome home, Agnes!" yelled George, who was sitting in back next to Richard.

I couldn't believe all three of them had piled in the car for the five-minute drive to pick me up. But I was kind of glad they had.

"Georgie's been dying to say that all day," said Mo, as if she'd taught him some special trick.

I snapped my seatbelt into the buckle. "Thanks, George."

Richard mumbled something, which I wondered if he'd practiced too.

"This is for you," added George.

He shoved his little hand under my hair. Something cold scratched my neck and I took it from his fingers.

"My very favorite button from my collection. I want you to have it."

It was navy blue with a little gold anchor in the middle.

"Wasn't that nice of Georgie!" Mo gushed. "He was trying to come up with the perfect gift for you and I think he nailed it."

I glanced back and noticed he wasn't wearing his butler jacket or using his phony butler voice.

"It's really cool," I said.

He grinned so hard, he squinted.

We pulled into the driveway beside our little beige house. The paint was still peeling in all the same spots and shingles were still missing from the roof. It really seemed as if nothing had changed, but in a way, everything had.

George jumped out of the car before I did, opened my door, and grabbed my hand. "Come on, Agnes! We have a much bigger present out back."

I glanced over at Mo, who was taking her time getting out of the driver's seat. "Hang on, Houdini," she hollered as she slammed the car door. "Richard and I want to watch."

I couldn't imagine what they had planned for me in the backyard, and I was a little afraid to find out.

"Cover your eyes," ordered George as he shoved me forward.

"No peeking!" added Mo.

After a few minutes of inching around the house, my hands blocking my view, George grabbed my elbow.

"Can I look?"

"Not yet," he said as he twisted me a little to the left.

"Now?"

George giggled and yelled, "Now!"

A sea of yellow sunflowers appeared in front of me, flowing across the field beyond our yard. Hundreds of them, framed by the setting sun. Enormous green stalks crowned with the most magnificent petals I had ever seen.

"Aren't they beautiful, Agnes?" said George.

"They really are," I whispered. "But how did they get here?"

Mo couldn't contain herself any longer. "Richard did it!"

I peered over at him and, for the first time since I'd met Richard, he grinned.

"When?" I asked.

"Your mom told me you wanted her to bring some back from Kansas," he replied, louder than his usual mumble, "so I bought a bunch of seed packets in town and planted them before we left for Topeka. They'll be fully grown in a month."

I didn't know what to say, so Mo said it for me.

"She loves them, Richard. Don't you, Agnes?"

I nodded. "They're wonderful. Thank you."

George let out a squeal. "You can hide in them too," he informed me, and then cupped his hands and yelled, "*Yoo-hoo!*"

At that moment I spotted a person ducking and winding through the forest of flowers, until she made her way out into the overgrown grass in front of us.

Viva.

Her hair was dyed purple and she wore overalls and work boots. "Hey squirt," she said, which is what she'd always called me, even though I was now taller than she was. "Surprise!"

Then she spread her arms.

I don't know if I ran over to her or if she ran to me, but once I reached her, I didn't want to let go.

"Where've you been?" I whispered into her ear, my cheeks already wet with tears.

She pulled me in tighter and I could feel her crying too. "I was lost for a while, but I'm home now."

All at once, Mo crushed us together with both arms. "The Moon girls, together again!"

Viva pulled back and wiped her face. "Hey, when did you become a giant, squirt?"

"She's a woman now too," Mo announced, as if it was her duty to inform everyone that I got my period.

I almost said something but rolled my eyes instead.

"No kidding?" said Viva. "Watch out, world!"

"Can we eat dinner?" George asked. Richard was holding him back, giving us some space. "I'm starving."

"Wash your hands, Georgie, and I'll set the table," said Mo. "Your father whipped up a feast. Are you two joining us?"

"In a few minutes," said Viva.

"Oh, I almost forgot." Mo grinned. "Megan's stopping by later with a batch of whoopee pies for dessert. So don't be long."

Then the three of them disappeared through the back door.

"Do you remember," said Viva, "how Mo would tell us to keep quiet or stay outside while Dad practiced before dinner?"

I did remember. How it used to annoy me to have to stop what I was doing so Dad could practice. But now I would give anything for things to go back to the way they were, even though I knew they never would.

"I used to love hearing Dad play his cello," she said. "It was the only time our family felt in harmony, like we were all part of the music."

The truth was, before the divorce, I used to love hearing him play too. "How do we feel that way again?" I asked.

She took my hand, something she used to do when I was little. "I'm not sure, squirt. But I think it starts with forgiving the people we love, especially ourselves."

I leaned against her shoulder.

The wind picked up and the golden blossoms swayed back and forth in the breeze, as if moving in harmony, together.

Acknowledgments

I am grateful to several people who contributed their knowledge and support to this novel. Many thanks to Anna Behuniak for her invaluable insights on growing up in a multicultural family. I would also like to thank Grae O'Toole, Lead Wildlife Keeper at the Vermont Institute for Natural Science, for answering my long list of questions about raptor rehabilitation. I'm also indebted to Kimberly Zieselman, Executive Director of InterACT, for her vital input and for the amazing work this organization does every day as Advocates for Intersex Youth. It was an honor to work again with editor Amy Fitzgerald, and the whole team at Lerner. As always, thank you to my agent and dear friend, Susan Cohen, for her years of devotion and phenomenal proofreading skills. And finally, my books are a family affair that I couldn't create without my son, Nathaniel Eames, my number one beta reader; my daughter, Madeleine Eames, a wonderful resource and sounding board; and my husband, Erik Eames, who continues to make all my dreams come true.

About the Author

Elizabeth Atkinson has been an editor, a children's librarian, an English teacher, and a newspaper columnist. Her passions, other than writing and keeping an eye out for fairies, include hiking, biking, snowshoeing, kayaking, traveling, and snooping. She divides her time between Newburyport, Massachusetts, and Lovell, Maine. Find out more at www.elizabethatkinson.com.